Bitter Sweet

Bitter Sweet

A Bitter Roots Mystery

C.J. Carmichael

Bitter Sweet

Copyright© 2019 C.J. Carmichael

Tule Publishing First Printing, July 2019

The Tule Publishing, Inc.

ALL RIGHTS RESERVED

First Publication by Tule Publishing 2019

Cover design by Croco Designs

No part of this book may be used or reproduced in any manner whatsoever without written permission except in the case of brief quotations embodied in critical articles and reviews.

This is a work of fiction. Names, characters, places, and incidents are products of the author's imagination or are used fictitiously. Any resemblance to actual events, locales, organizations, or persons, living or dead, is entirely coincidental.

ISBN: 978-1-951190-09-5

Dedication

For my first and beloved grandchild,
Owen Rupert Binnion Klein

Welcome to the County of Lost Trail, Montana
Pop. 2,859

Sheriff's Department

Zak Waller: the young, new sheriff. Lives in a basement apartment with his cat and has been dating Nadine Black for over a year.

Nadine Black: former barrel racer who now works as a deputy. Recently she took on the added role of coroner. Lives on an acreage with her horse and dog. Dating Zak Waller.

Kenny Bombard: former backcountry ski guide and Christmas tree farm manager, he is Lost Trail's newest deputy and is dating Tiff Masterson.

Beatrice Rollins: former school secretary is now the department's new dispatcher. She's married to a local rancher and has two grown children.

Masterson Family

Rosemary Masterson: inherited the Raven Christmas Tree Farm from her parents. She lives there with her adult daughterTiffany.

Irving Masterson: Rosemary's husband managed the farm until his death over seventeen years ago.

Marsha Masterson: Rosemary's sister, worked as a nurse at the Lost Trail Medical Clinic. Moved in with her sister after Irving's death. Now deceased.

Tiffany Masterson: Rosemary and Irving's daughter. Manages the farm and is dating Kenny Bombard. Close childhood friends with Zak Waller.

Casey Masterson: Tiff's older brother was born with a heart defect and died at the age of twelve.

Pittman Family

Clark Pittman: Was the local physician until a scandal forced him to retire.

Franny Pittman: Clark's wife died when their son, Justin, was six years old.

Justin Pittman: Local attorney, cancer survivor and adopted father of *Geneva.*

Chapter One

May 2

SYBIL TOMBE SHOULD have turned and run the moment she saw the finished crossword on her kitchen table, curls of dried orange peel beside it. But her mind was elsewhere, mulling over the anonymous letter she'd received at work that day.

She'd opened the mail in the lull after the preschool reading circle, the chatter and laughter of children still echoing off the library walls.

The brief sentences brought a chill to the room. She'd shivered. Felt a stab of panic. Then told herself it was impossible.

She'd read the note again. It must be some sort of prank. To be on the safe side, maybe she should show it to Zak Waller—the town's new sheriff—he had good instincts about these things. She'd see how she felt about it in the morning. For the time being, she shoved it into the bottom drawer of her desk.

A few customers came and went in the early afternoon. A new shipment of books arrived at the same time as a group of teenaged girls, whose teachers had asked them to read a book of their choice and write a review to share with the class.

"Can you help us find something interesting?" one of the girls asked.

"And short," another added.

Giggles.

Sybil and her best friend Rosemary Masterson had been like them once, bonded by shared secrets and laughter and blooming desires. Now approaching sixty, they were still friends, but the giggles were rare.

Frankly Sybil's giggles had been rare for a long time.

Since she'd moved back to Lost Trail, in her midtwenties to be precise. She'd wondered if people would see the change in her. Remarkably they hadn't. Or was it so remarkable? The longer she lived, the more Sybil understood how essentially self-centered most people were. Not from unkindness so much as the routine worries and busyness of their own lives.

At closing time Sybil went through the usual routine, powering down the computers, making sure the coffee machine was off and—most importantly—inspecting every room in the two-story structure, all the nooks and crannies, making sure no solitary reader, ensnared in a spellbinding tale, was accidently locked in for the night.

The early May day was still sunny and warm as she stepped onto the porch at six o'clock. Looked like the rainy spell was finally over. One door over, Debbie-Ann Prince was locking up her Little Cow Pokes Day Care, her young daughter waiting patiently beside her.

"Thanks for the story circle today. Thursdays are my easiest days thanks to you."

"My pleasure. I love having all the little ones around." In Sybil's opinion, Debbie-Ann, the sunny-natured single mom who'd started her day care business six months after Ashley's birth, deserved all the help she got.

Sybil checked to make sure the dead bolt was engaged, then tucked her key in the special zipper compartment of her purse. Debbie-Ann and Ashley had set off north on Second Street, probably toward Justin Pittman's house. Debbie-Ann and Justin—the town's only lawyer—spent a lot of time together. Something was brewing there, for sure.

Rosemary—who had recently discovered she was Justin's biological mother—would be pleased. The past few years had been hard on Justin. Hopefully the success of his stem-cell transplant marked the beginning of happier times.

Sybil appreciated the vibrant green of the grass and the budding new leaves as she walked the block and a half to Natural Grocers. For dinner tonight she was going to make coconut red lentil dahl, a big batch so she could put some in the freezer. At the checkout line she chatted with Elaine Cobbles about the weather and how everyone would be anxious to put in their gardens now that the rain had finally stopped.

Such an ordinary day. A day like thousands of others.

She'd seen nothing unusual about her modest bungalow

as she approached her front door. She'd let herself in with her key, removed her shoes and set down her purse and the groceries before heading to her office to check her computer, where she hoped to find a message confirming plans for Sunday.

But she'd no sooner logged onto the site than a creak from the kitchen stopped her. She hesitated, cocked her head, wondered if she'd imagined the sound.

She decided to investigate. As soon as she crossed the threshold, she spotted the foreign objects among her everyday clutter: extra reading glasses, a box of tissues, a withering poinsettia plant she hadn't yet given up on.

She should have known. The crossword. The orange peels. Slowly her brain worked to build the necessary connections…and then she saw the teddy bear propped next to the toaster on her counter.

And suddenly the meaning of these things was crystal clear.

There was the sound of breaking glass. And then an arm grabbed at her waist, pulling her back into a solid mass of muscle and bone. Briefly she inhaled the smell of unwashed hair, perspiration.

His other arm snaked around her neck in a relentless chokehold.

She heard her name as she gasped for breath.

"Are you happy to see me?"

Black spots danced in her eyes. Her vision narrowed.

And then nothing.

Chapter Two

May 3

"SHERIFF? WE MAY have a problem. No one seems to know where our librarian is."

The phone call from his dispatcher was almost a relief to Zak Waller, since it gave him a reason to set aside the financial spreadsheets he'd been working on since leaving the office at noon. According to the schedule, he got Friday afternoons off. It never worked out that way though, and he had the headache to prove it.

"Tell me more, Bea." Pacing, with his phone to his ear, Zak kicked a pair of socks out of his path. His cat, Watson, who'd been sleeping on the sofa, glanced at the socks. At one time he would have pounced and batted at anything that moved, but he was getting older. He yawned, then went back to sleep.

"Debbie-Ann called from her day care. She said Sybil hasn't opened the library today. She tried phoning both the library and Sybil's cell phone—no answer at either number."

Beatrix Rollins, the dispatcher Zak hired after he took up his new post, had a gift for stating facts clearly and succinctly. The fifty-two-year-old former school secretary was also organized and not afraid to take the initiative.

Helpful qualities in a four-person sheriff's office.

"Was Sybil at the library yesterday?"

"Yes. Debbie-Ann saw her at the morning reading circle, then again at six when they were both closing up for the day."

"Probably Sybil is home sick?"

"That's what Debbie-Ann thought. On her suggestion I called Sybil's neighbor, Ellie Somers—she used to teach kindergarten?—and Ellie went over to check the house. She tried knocking but she didn't get an answer. Ellie knows where Sybil keeps her spare key, but when she looked under the garden gnome on Sybil's back deck it wasn't there."

"So, she hasn't searched the house?" Zak pictured the small, cheerful bungalow. Lavender-blue wood siding with pale yellow trim and a front garden blooming with color every summer.

"Well, she sort of did. Turns out the curtains were all open, so Ellie looked in the windows. She's almost positive Sybil isn't inside. Her car is still parked in the garage though."

That was strange. "We'll follow up with some calls to Sybil's closest friends. Rosemary Masterson—"

"Yes, Sheriff, I called Rosemary," Bea continued. "Last time she spoke to Sybil was yesterday afternoon, on the phone. Sybil confirmed she was going to their book club meeting, which is happening tonight at Rosemary's. According to Rosemary, Sybil sounded fine and didn't say anything about any plans to leave town."

Sybil was a reliable and punctual woman who took her duties as the town librarian seriously. If she hadn't shown up for work, there had to be a good reason.

"She usually gets someone to post a note on the library door if she can't get to work," he recalled.

"That's true. I remember seeing those notes. Not that Sybil gets sick very often. Maybe she had to make an unexpected trip?"

"Didn't you say her car is still in the garage?"

"Someone might have picked her up…? But then there would be a note on the library door. Sybil would never leave without telling anyone." Bea made a frustrated clicking sound.

"Yes." The next step was obvious, which made Zak wonder why he'd been called.

"You better ask Nadine to swing by the house."

"She's still on patrol. Says she's at least an hour away."

Nadine had been spending so much time driving the far reaches of the county lately she was beginning to remind him of Butterfield, who'd gone into retirement after Zak became sheriff.

"And of course, it's Kenny's day off," Bea continued. "Want me to call him in?"

Zak was already sticking his feet into his boots. "Nope.

I'm on my way. In the meantime, can you phone Rosemary back and ask her to make a list of Sybil's friends and business associates? Anyone who might know where she is. Once she has the list, help her contact them all."

"Absolutely, Sheriff."

Though he was worried about Sybil, Zak wasn't sorry to set aside his computer and papers. The budget—due to be approved in July—was driving him crazy. No matter how hard he tried, he could not find a way to fund the extra deputy they needed so badly. Not without compromising on training courses—something he couldn't do with his young, inexperienced staff.

Zak wondered if the citizens of Lost Trail had known what they were doing when they kicked out long-time incumbent Sheriff Ford and elected him, instead. He'd been with the department only four years—and most of that time had been spent as dispatcher. True, he'd managed to solve three homicides during that time but there was a lot more than investigative work involved in being sheriff.

His staff was equally green. His most senior deputy, who also happened to be his girlfriend, Nadine Black, had been working in law enforcement for only a few years and had just taken on the local coroner duties as well. She was stretched to the max.

Which left Kenny Bouchard, a former ski guide and Christmas tree farm operator Zak had hired on as deputy three months ago, about two weeks before he hired Bea.

Zak had faith in his team; everyone was dedicated and smart. With a few more years' experience they'd be top notch. It was surviving those few years that was going to be tough. As it was, Zak was working eighty-hour weeks and his normal ten-mile runs, five days a week, had tapered to one five-mile run a week, if he was lucky.

Worse than the impact on his fitness routine, was the toll his new job was taking on his relationship with Nadine. Recently he'd noticed Nadine watching him as if she was trying to figure out how to tell him something.

When she finally found the words, he was afraid he wasn't going to like them.

But what could he do? The citizens of Lost Trail had elected him sheriff. He couldn't let them down.

As he collected his badge, wallet and keys, Watson jumped up to the window ledge, his usual perch when he sensed Zak was about to leave.

One whiff of the fresh spring air had Zak longing to throw on his running shoes and head for the trails. He hadn't been out for so long his running buddy, Luke Stillman, had given up texting him. He wondered when, if ever, life would get back to normal.

Though Sybil lived only five or six blocks away, Zak drove. Trading in his old truck for Ford's new Chevy Tahoe had been one of the perks of the new job. He aimed it for Sybil's home, on the north end of town, backing onto the forest that surrounded Lost Creek Park.

From the street, nothing looked amiss. He checked the front door, which was locked as Ellie Somers had reported, and peered in the windows at the entryway and the living room.

On the floor by the entrance was a purse, a bag of groceries and a pair of shoes, which made it seem that Sybil had made it home after Debbie-Ann saw her lock up the library Thursday at six.

He loped to the back of the house, pausing to look into the window of a room that was obviously Sybil's bedroom. He couldn't see the far corners, but he did have a good view of the bed, which had been made. Another room, the office, also appeared vacant.

The back door was locked. None of the windows appeared tampered with, though the one over the kitchen sink had been left unlocked and slightly ajar.

He spotted the gnome Bea had mentioned and turned it over.

Nothing.

He tried other possible hiding places: under the back mat, the top of window ledges, inside her propane barbecue. With mounting unease, he called Rosemary Masterson. Her daughter, Tiff, happened to be a good friend of his, so he knew Rosemary well.

"Hey Rosemary. I'm at Sybil's house and I can't find the spare key to her house."

"Have you looked under the garden gnome?"

"Yes. It's not there."

"That's odd. Since she lives alone Sybil has a fear of locking herself out of her own house. She's kind of paranoid about having that spare key close to hand." Rosemary sounded concerned.

"Maybe she lent the key to someone?"

"I can't think why she would do that. Or why she isn't answering her phone." She paused. "You don't suppose she fell and knocked herself out? The stairs to her basement are awfully steep."

"I'm wondering the same thing." Something on the kitchen floor caught his attention. A pool of dried, red liquid. His heartbeat quickened.

"Call me if you hear anything. I've got to go." Keeping his gaze on the stain, he tucked his phone in his back pocket and made his way to the unlocked window. From this closer view the stain still appeared reddish, viscous.

He had to go in.

Zak pulled on gloves, then grasped the sides of the dusty screen and eased it from the frame. After that all he had to do was lift the window up another twenty inches or so.

"Sybil? You home? This is Zak Waller from the sheriff's department. I'm coming in."

The house absorbed his words and gave nothing back.

Zak heaved himself up and then wriggled, headfirst through the opening. He reached past the kitchen sink for the counter, crawling forward until his entire body was inside. Then he sprang to the floor and scanned the room.

No sign of Sybil.

He moved to the pool of red liquid and could see right away it wasn't blood. That was good, but it still left him with questions. It didn't stand to reason that Sybil would have left a mess like this on her kitchen floor if she had any say in the matter.

He knelt by the stain and inhaled deeply. Some kind of spicy tomato juice maybe? A few feet from the splattered liquid—blocked from view of the kitchen window by a cabinet—lay a shattered drinking glass.

Had something or someone startled Sybil here in the kitchen, causing her to drop this glass?

"Sybil!" He called out her name again without any expectation of an answer. The house had a hollow, empty feel to it. Still, he needed to be sure Sybil wasn't lying hurt or unconscious somewhere. He opened the door to the basement and flicked on the light.

The staircase was unobstructed.

He hurried down the steps.

The dank, airless smell transported him back in time to games of hide-and-seek in his grandparents' basement. His older brothers had loved to torment him by making spooky noises and jumping out from dark corners.

He walked past the washer and dryer and laundry sink. Some sweaters were spread on towels on a stainless-steel rack. As he walked by, he touched one of the sweaters—it was cherry red. He remembered Sybil wearing it. Dry.

There were no doors down here and he could take in the entire space without walking farther. The furnace, hot water tank, and electric panel were on the far end of the basement. To the left of the laundry setup were stacked plastic storage boxes and a set of downhill skis.

That was it.

He raced back up the stairs and quickly searched the rest of the two-bedroom bungalow.

No sign of Sybil anywhere.

The toilet seat in the single bathroom was up. He considered that for a few moments, then went to the foyer. Sybil's purse gapped open enough for him to see that her wallet and cell phone were both inside. The canvas grocery bag contained lentils, canned coconut milk, a sweet potato.

The receipt in the bag was dated yesterday, shortly after she'd closed the library at six.

Why hadn't she put the groceries away? What had interrupted her? It seemed safe to assume the spilled juice and broken glass had to be connected.

Zak went back to the kitchen. Inside the fridge were enough groceries to suggest Sybil hadn't been planning to go anywhere. Lots of fresh fruit and veggies, including an open box of vegetable cocktail juice.

Zak closed the fridge then surveyed the floor. This time he noticed a small amount of the juice had been tracked across the floor. He dropped to his hands and knees. The tracks looked like they were from the heel of a large-sized work boot. Most likely a man's boot.

Zak inspected the rest of the room again. Some clutter on the table—reading glasses, tissues, a newspaper and some dried orange peels beside it.

The newspaper—Saturday's *New York Times*—was open to the crossword section. And it was completed. He noted the heavy, right-slanted letters. Picking up the paper he went to compare the printing to the grocery list stuck to the fridge.

That printing was light, with upright, rounded letters.

The crossword had been completed by someone other than Sybil. Probably the same man who'd left the toilet seat up and tracked the spilled juice with his boots.

Sybil had no male relatives or boyfriend that he knew of. So, who was this guy? And had he been an invited guest…or an intruder?

The length of time Sybil had been missing—almost twenty-four hours—the missing house key, and Sybil's purse at the front door made him suspect intruder. Women didn't leave home willingly without their purse, wallet or cell phone. And most wouldn't leave a glass of spilled juice on the floor except in an emergency.

And if it had been an emergency, surely by now she would have gotten in touch with someone to let them know she was okay.

An intruder wouldn't have had a hard time finding her

spare key. The garden gnome would have been one of the first places he checked.

Once inside the man could have passed time waiting for Sybil by doing the crossword and possibly eating that orange. When Sybil finally came home, the man startled her, or possibly even attacked her, in the process knocking over that glass of juice.

And then…? There was no evidence Sybil had been seriously harmed here in the kitchen. But she could have been forcibly removed. The backyard was screened by tall trees, so it would have been possible for someone to force her to walk—or carry her—to a waiting vehicle.

Zak left the way he'd come in, through the window, making sure to leave the place just as he'd found it. He checked the garage, which was locked, but through a window he was able to confirm Sybil's sedan was still inside.

He walked around the garage and inspected the graveled driveway. There'd been a lot of rain last week and he could see fresh tire tracks leading up to Sybil's garage. The tracks stopped a foot shy of the garage.

He took a few pictures on his phone. From the size and tread he guessed they'd been made by a midsized pickup truck with all-season tires. Definitely not the small sedan inside Sybil's garage.

He was reaching for his phone when he heard footsteps behind him. Turning he spotted a thin, small-framed woman, possibly in her seventies, with fluffy yellow hair—

obviously dyed—and an alert, curious manner.

"Sheriff, I'm glad to see you. I've been so worried about Sybil. I take it you've been in her house and haven't found her?"

Zak nodded. "Don't think we've met. I'm Sheriff Waller."

She shook his hand. "I'm Ellie Somers. I've lived across the street from Sybil forever. I tell you, she's a woman who sticks to her routine and this…disappearance…just doesn't make sense."

"When's the last time you saw Sybil?"

Ellie shrugged her slender shoulders. "It's been a few days. I noticed the lights were off in her house yesterday evening. I assumed she must be out with friends. Sybil has a lot of friends."

"She say anything to you about taking time off work? Going on a trip, maybe?"

"No. It's been life as usual. Though I have noticed her taking more day trips than usual on Sundays." Ellie raised her thin, penciled-in brows. "I thought maybe she found herself a fella. About time."

"Have you noticed any men visiting her here at home?"

"No," Ellie admitted with obvious disappointment. "Sybil is a sociable woman, but she doesn't entertain in her own house. Usually she goes out." After a few seconds Ellie added, "Though I did see a man in a pickup truck turn into her driveway around three o'clock yesterday. I was watching

Jeopardy before going out to the community center to play Scrabble with the Go-Getters."

Zak recognized the name of the seniors' organization. "Did you get a good look at this man?"

"He was wearing a cowboy hat, and he had a beard, so I couldn't see much of his face."

"What about the truck itself? Can you tell me the make and color?"

"I'm not good with vehicles, Sheriff. It was one of those big, four-door cab pickups. As for color, it was so dirty it was hard to tell. Could have been black or gray, or even dark blue, I suppose."

After all the rain it wasn't necessarily suspicious that the truck was dirty. But a good splashing of mud could provide cover for anyone with criminal intentions.

"Did you see the truck leave?"

"No. To tell you the truth, I figured he must have been turning around. We do live at a dead end, so it happens a lot."

"But you didn't actually see him turn around?"

"No. My show was just ending and my mind was on other things. It was my turn to bring cookies for our coffee and I'd forgotten to take them out of the freezer." Ellie twisted her hands. "Do you think that man knew Sybil? Did he take her somewhere?"

"It's too soon to say. Thanks for your help, Mrs. Somers. If you think of anything else, let us know immediately.

Someone will be contacting you shortly to get your official statement."

Adrenaline zipped through Zak's veins…similar to the high he felt before a big race, providing the fuel he needed to go the distance. And the distance here was vast.

He needed to get a warrant. Search the house, her desk at the library. Get castings of these tracks while they were fresh. Put out word with the state police.

It was possible there was an innocent explanation for Sybil's absence, but Zak's instincts suggested otherwise.

Chapter Three

DEPUTY NADINE BLACK was relieved to be out on patrol. Not because, after two weeks of constant rain, the countryside was looking brighter and greener than it would all year, but because it meant she could avoid the scrutiny of her boyfriend—and boss—Sheriff Zak Waller.

Zak knew something was up. She'd sensed an unspoken question yesterday after work when he asked if he could come over and cook her dinner.

It was something he did more nights than not, and she couldn't recall a single time she'd turned down his offer. Not just because she loved the guy, but because she hated to cook.

When she'd said, "Maybe not. I'm kind of tired," his eyebrows had shot up, but he hadn't voiced the question in his eyes.

They needed to talk—it was her nature to speak her mind—but finding the right time would be tricky. Since being elected sheriff, Zak, who had always been devoted to his job, had become obsessed. She couldn't blame him, in his boots she would do the same.

But it put her in a tough situation.

Stop thinking, she commanded herself. Enjoy the scenery and focus on your job.

She rarely patrolled this area since it was so sparsely populated. At the boundary road that ran along the forest reserve linking Lost Trail to neighboring Beaverhead County, she turned right and drove for twenty minutes without seeing anything but rolling hills and ponderosa pines.

This county of theirs, enveloped by mountains and forests, was one of the least populated in all of America. The mountain pass that connected them to the rest of Montana could be dangerous to drive in the winter. Sometimes, during a bad blizzard, they would be cut off for a week or more.

The adversity required people to be tough and self-sufficient. Though she'd grown up in a more populated, urban area of Montana, Nadine liked to think she shared these qualities. Almost a decade on the rodeo circuit had a way of putting steel in a woman's backbone.

Which made her current state of limbo so intolerable.

She was a woman of action—give her something to do and she'd be right on it.

But relationships didn't work that way. They required conversations, compromises and concessions. Not exactly her skill set.

She gripped and regripped the steering wheel of her truck. Normally she'd be thrilled by the view of the Bitterroot Mountains ahead of her. A lot less snow on those peaks than there'd been just a few weeks ago. Wildflowers bloomed in the ditch on either side of her, masses and masses of arrowleaf balsamroot carpeting the woods with their golden beauty.

But the questions wouldn't go away. What was she going to do? When was she going to tell him?

The road dipped and suddenly she was on a long, flat stretch. A cultivated field to her right stretched out into the distance. After a while she spotted the farmer, in his big green tractor, pulling a cultivator through the rich, dark soil.

On her next day off she wanted to start working on her own garden, too. Now that she owned an acreage, she was excited to grow potatoes, green peas, tomatoes…

A line of cultivated maple trees came into view, six mature trees that led from the road to a weathered farmhouse with a rusted metal roof. Nadine eased off the gas pedal. Ahead of the house, not far from the road, a woman worked a large vegetable patch.

The wife of the farmer she'd just passed?

The woman was tall, large, with thick auburn hair braided down her back.

On impulse Nadine pulled her truck to the shoulder.

The woman dropped her hoe and reached for a large sweatshirt draped over a wheelbarrow at the end of the row. It covered not only her T-shirt but fell halfway down her baggy jeans as well.

"Hi there." Nadine left her truck and started for the lane. In the tall grass by the road, dragonflies looped and darted, hunting down the season's first crop of mosquitoes. "Could I bother you for a glass of water? I usually bring some when I'm out on patrol but today I forgot."

The woman looked to be barely eighteen, if that. She had deep-set eyes, freckles on her nose, an uncertain smile.

"Um, sure. I could get you some water. I wouldn't mind a drink either. It's hot out here today."

"Sure is." Nadine pushed her sunglasses higher up the bridge of her nose. Why had the young woman been in such a hurry to pull on that sweatshirt when she was obviously hot and sweaty? Embarrassed about her weight? "I'm Deputy Black."

That earned her a smile, which was pretty despite a slight crossbite.

"I'm Amber Woodrow. We could have our drink on the porch if you want?"

The question was asked as if Amber expected to be turned down, and Nadine felt a pang for the young girl. It had to be dreadfully lonely living so far from the nearest neighbor and over an hour from town. "Gladly."

She joined Amber on the maple-lined road, noting the girl's rounded shoulders and stiff arms. Nadine, tall herself, fought the urge to tell the girl to straighten her spine and be proud of her size.

Instead she commented on the maples. "Bet those trees

turn a gorgeous red in the autumn."

"They do. My mom planted them right after she married my father. She grew up in Vermont. She always said when it came to natural beauty Montana would be perfect, if only there were maples."

Nadine picked up on the wistful tone. "Is your mom…?"

Amber nodded. "She passed away three winters ago."

A dog jogged stiffly to meet them, a yellow Lab, graying at the muzzle, a roll of fat at his neck. Nadine bent to give him a pat as Amber continued to the house. "I'll be right out with something to drink. You still want water? I've got lemonade, too."

"Lemonade would be awesome if it's not too much trouble."

Amber's answering smile inferred it wasn't. Overall, Nadine had the impression Amber was glad of the interruption—and break—from gardening.

Being a nosy person by nature and profession, Nadine would have preferred to get a look inside the house. The vintage log home gave the impression of being a little neglected from the outside. The oak barrel planters flanking the front door had probably been filled with red geraniums when Amber's mother was alive, rather than the weeds growing there now.

The welcome mat was so dirty, it could barely be read, and the windows and screens were grimy too.

In little more than a minute Amber was back with a tray

containing two glasses and a pitcher of lemonade. Thankfully the glasses looked clean.

"Was that your father I saw on the tractor back there?" Nadine pointed in the direction she'd driven from.

Amber lowered her gaze. "Yes. He's getting ready to plant the wheat."

"Do you have any brothers or sisters?"

"A brother. He lives in Great Falls. Has a job with an insurance company."

So, it was just Amber and her father living out here, miles from the closest neighbor. "How old are you, Amber? To be honest, you look young enough to be in school."

"I quit after grade ten. I'm seventeen now."

Nadine wasn't sure how to respond to that troublesome answer. Had Amber wanted to quit school so early? Did she have any plans for her life other than helping her dad on the family farm?

Unless Amber was being neglected or abused, none of this was any of her business.

Before she could continue the conversation, Amber tilted her head and gave her a shy smile. "Do you mind me asking your first name? Is it Nadine?"

She pulled back, then smiled. "Don't tell me you recognize me?"

"Sure do. I've watched you on YouTube more times than I can count. Mom used to take us to all the local rodeos. I was real disappointed when I heard you retired. You were kind of like my hero."

Wow. Who knew she'd find a fan out here on the edge of the wilderness? "Do you ride?" There was a paddock next to the barn, but she couldn't see any horses, or livestock of any kind.

"I did." Amber lowered her gaze to her glass. "Dad sold the horses after Mom died. He said I was getting too fat to ride, anyway."

"Well, that's a load of crap." How could a father speak to his daughter that way?

When Amber stayed quiet, Nadine realized she had probably been too frank. "Sorry. I shouldn't have said that. I'm just sensitive because at your age I was a lot taller...and, shall we say, more solid...than most of the other girls my age. My mom taught me to be proud of my body." She stopped. "I'm talking too much again."

"That's okay. I agree with you. My dad was a lot nicer when Mom was alive." Amber pulled on her sleeves as she talked, stretching them over her hands so barely the tips of her fingers were showing.

The girl was like a turtle trying to crawl into its shell. Yet she seemed to want to talk. "Your mother's death must have been hard for all of you."

"Yeah. Dad sold all her stuff. And he started drinking. He and my brother got into so many arguments Ian finally moved away."

"You ever think of moving away?"

"Maybe when I'm eighteen."

Nadine wasn't sure how far she should prod. "You say your dad used to argue with your brother. Does he argue with you too? Maybe, sometimes…hurt you?"

"I'm sorry," Amber cut her off. "I didn't mean to complain about my father. He's okay. Living here is fine. It's a bit isolated, but I have my escapes. Books. My dad and I go to town every week and I always stop at the library and stock up on novels."

Okay, so no more talk about the father. "I like to read too. What kind of stories are your favorite?"

"Oh, romance, definitely. Especially the ones about ranchers and cowboys. Sybil always sets aside a stack for me. She knows exactly what I like."

"She's a great librarian, for sure," Nadine agreed.

"I love the ones about rodeo cowboys and cowgirls best. What was it like being a barrel racer? Do you miss it?"

Nadine stayed another ten minutes, answering Amber's questions about her former life in rodeo. To her surprise, Amber even brought out an old rodeo program for her to sign.

When her phone buzzed, Nadine pulled it out of her pocket and glanced at the screen. Seeing the message, she felt guilty for having lingered.

"I'm needed back at the office." Nadine set down her empty glass. "Thanks a lot, Amber. I enjoyed talking with you. I have some old romance books I'll probably never read again. Next time I'm out this way I'll drop them off for you."

"Really?" Her eyes brightened, then she glanced over Nadine's shoulder and her smile faltered. "It's okay if you forget. You must be super busy." She dropped her eyes and began tugging on her sleeves again.

As she hurried back to her vehicle, Nadine wondered what had made Amber go from excited to nervous so quickly. Was she worried someone might not approve of Nadine coming by again? Someone being her father, or perhaps a controlling boyfriend?

Nadine couldn't help feeling concerned about this girl. She said she was doing fine. But that didn't explain the bruises on her wrists or why she was working so hard to hide them.

Chapter Four

"I'M WORRIED ABOUT Sybil."

That's interesting, Mom. Because I'm worried about you. Tiff Masterson swiveled her chair away from the computer so she could face her mother. "Why?"

"Bea called from the sheriff's office. Sybil didn't open the library this morning. No one's seen her since closing time yesterday at six."

Tiff absentmindedly took a cookie from the container her mother had brought from the house. Her mother—who treated everyone employed by Raven Christmas Tree Farm like they were family—had already offered them to the men working outside. Thanks to the good weather, Bob Jenkins and his crew of three were finally able to plant trees this week. They were trying a new variety this year, the Canaan fir. It was a bit of a risk because no one knew how the West Virginia native would withstand the harsh Montana winters.

Tiff had discussed the risk with her mother, but uncharacteristically her mom had seemed uninterested. She'd said she trusted Tiff and had left it like that.

Something else was on her mother's mind. Something

that was causing her sleepless nights and an unusual air of preoccupation.

Tiff's mom cleared her throat.

"Sorry. Maybe Sybil's sick. Or had errands to run in Hamilton."

"She isn't home, and her car's in her garage. Plus, she didn't leave a note on the library door. She always does that if she can't open the library as usual."

"Maybe she was feeling too sick to do that. Could be she asked a neighbor to drive her to the medical clinic."

Since the closure of the local Lost Trail clinic, the nearest one was in Hamilton. Driving there and back would take up a big chunk of a day.

"That doesn't explain why she isn't answering any calls or text messages on her cell phone. I've been trying to reach her for hours." Her mother's voice quavered. "The sheriff's office has been notified. Something's wrong. I know it."

Tiff didn't know what to think. Sybil was a fixture in Lost Trail. It seemed impossible something bad had happened to her. Sybil was kind, thoughtful, stable…the sort of person you turned to in times of trouble.

Sybil had been a loyal friend to her mom during some very trying times. It would be awful if something bad had happened to her. But what were the chances of that?

"There has to be a simple solution. I'm sure they'll find her soon." She had absolute confidence in Zak and his team of deputies—which now included her boyfriend Kenny

Bombard.

But until they did, her mom would worry. Tiff couldn't let her do it on her own. "Tell you what, I'll come back to the house with you. We can phone around town."

"I've already made a list of people. Bea Rollins called and asked me. So far I've talked to everyone in our book club. No luck."

Tiff knew there was a book club meeting scheduled at their place that evening. "Sybil was planning to come?"

"As of yesterday, she was."

"Then I'm sure she'll be here." Tiff squeezed her mom's shoulder gently. "I need to pay an important bill and then I'll lock up the office and meet you back at the house. Shouldn't take more than fifteen minutes."

"Thanks, honey." Her mom went to the door, then paused to look back at the room she was exiting. Her lips curved in a faint, sad smile. This had once been her father's office. Then her husband's. So many memories.

Tiff had them too. She never sat at this desk without picturing her father, leaning back in the leather chair, stretching out his arms to rest his hands possessively on the scarred walnut desk. What would he think about her taking over the farm? She hoped he'd be proud.

Once her mother was gone, Tiff texted Kenny. He wasn't scheduled to work this afternoon, but maybe he'd heard something.

Sybil Tombe is missing?

Within a minute he called her.

"Hey, Tiff. I just heard from Zak. He needs me to head over to Sybil's and get a casting of some tire tracks in her driveway."

This sounded serious. A chill ran down her back. "What do you think happened to her?"

"Our investigation is just starting. All we know for sure is that she's been missing almost twenty-four hours and none of her friends or neighbors have a clue where she could be. Once we get a warrant, we'll conduct a proper search of her house and the library. Hopefully we'll learn more after that."

Oh crap. Her mom had been right to worry. "Are you sure that's all you know? I'm no cop but I doubt if you can get a warrant to search someone's house just because no one has seen them for a day."

"Huh. Has anyone ever told you it's annoying to be too smart?"

Fortunately Kenny wasn't the kind of guy to be intimidated by a brainy woman. "So what evidence did you find?"

"Sorry, babe. I'm not at liberty to share that."

"Really? What good is it having a deputy as a boyfriend if I can't get the inside scoop?"

"I like to think I have my uses."

She smiled, then told him about her and her mother's plan to call everyone they could think of.

"That would be really helpful. Let me know if you learn anything."

"I definitely will."

In a lower voice Kenny asked, "We still on for later tonight?"

She felt a happy glow. Ever since Kenny stopped working and living at Raven Farm, their relationship had been so much better. "Mom's got her book club coming tonight. So, yes, I'll be at the Dew Drop by seven. Can't wait."

AT THREE FORTY-FIVE Bea routed a call to Zak's office phone. He'd just finished the paperwork for the warrant and gave the form a quick scan as he said, "Sheriff Waller here."

It was Carolyne Elgin, the principal at the elementary school.

"A little girl in the third grade reported seeing a man watching her at recess this afternoon. For some reason she didn't tell her teacher until the end of the school day, and I just found out about it now. It's probably nothing, but I wanted to tell you." Carolyne cleared her throat. "Just in case."

Hell. When it rains it pours. He'd never had two serious reports in one day before.

"Thanks. You did the right thing. We'll need to interview the girl." If Nadine was back from patrol, he'd send her. The girl might feel more comfortable with a woman, besides he was anxious to get this warrant approved and start a serious search of Sybil's house. The laptop open on her desk would be his first target.

"Her mother picked her up fifteen minutes ago. If you want to come in tomorrow morning—"

"No. We need to talk to her tonight. While her memory is fresh."

"Fair enough. The girl is Darby Larkin."

"Chris and Patsy's kid?"

"That's correct."

Zak changed his plan. Patsy owned the Snowdrift Café in town, and after this crazy afternoon, he could really use a coffee and a muffin. He'd get Nadine to finalize the warrant. He'd interview the Larkin girl.

Zak stood from his desk and stretched his arms. Last few weeks he'd noticed the waist of his pants getting a little tight. If he wasn't careful, he was going to end up with a potbelly like old Sheriff Ford's.

Scratch the muffin, he'd better stick to the coffee. On his way out the door he dropped his paperwork on Bea's desk. "When Nadine gets back from patrol, get her to handle this pronto." He paused, then added, "Aren't you supposed to be off this afternoon?"

"Don't worry. I won't put in for overtime. But I'd rather be here making myself useful than home worrying about Sybil."

He could see the concern in her eyes. "Are you and Sybil friends?"

"We went to grade school together. I lost touch with her when she went off to college, but once she came back and opened the library, we reconnected. And I use the library a lot. Sybil's like an institution in this town. We owe it to her to find her."

Zak felt the same. He might not have an official degree in criminology, but thanks to Sybil, he'd read all the books.

BUSINESS WAS SLOW at the Snowdrift. No lineup at the counter, just one customer sitting in the back corner, working on his laptop. Zak went to the display case and eyed the peach scones wistfully. Patsy made awesome scones.

"Hey, Zak." Patsy came out from the kitchen, drying her hands on the white apron that covered her plaid shirt and skinny jeans. Her light brown hair was pulled back into a braid long enough to rest on one shoulder. She had an open face, round gray eyes, and the windblown complexion you got from skiing every chance you got all winter. The Larkins were all keen downhill skiers.

"Need an afternoon caffeine boost?" she asked.

"Always."

"Want a scone to go with that?"

"I'd love one but I better not." He lowered his voice. "I need to talk to you and Darby. Did your daughter tell you what happened at school today?"

"You mean the old guy at recess?" Patsy filled a large paper cup with coffee and passed it to him. "Pretty creepy. You got any idea who he is?"

Zak handed over money for the drink. "Not yet. I'm hoping Darby can give me a description."

"Hang on, she's back in the kitchen, supposed to be helping me bake cookies, but she's spending more time on my iPad."

"I wouldn't have to share yours if I had my own, Mom."

Zak grinned.

"Like that's going to happen. Come out here, Darby. Sheriff Waller wants to talk to you."

Moments later a mini version of Patsy—long hair in a braid, same round, gray eyes—came out through the passageway.

"Did Trevor do something wrong again?"

A few years ago, her brother had been caught breaking his curfew and engaging in Halloween vandalism. In so doing Trevor had become an important witness in the first homicide case Zak had ever solved.

"Hi there, Darby. Nobody's done anything wrong," Zak said. "I just had a call from your principal. Mrs. Elgin told me you noticed something unusual at recess this afternoon. Can you tell me about it?"

Darby let out a long-suffering sigh. "I already told my teacher. And Mom."

"Just one more time, honey." Patsy put a hand on her

daughter's shoulder. "Let's sit at the table by the window. Sure you don't want a scone, Sheriff?"

"I would!" Darby raised her eyebrows hopefully.

Patsy put her hands on her hips. Zak could sense a refusal coming and saw a chance to earn some points with the little girl.

"Maybe we could share one?"

Patsy tipped her head from one side to the other. "I suppose. But only if you have a glass of milk with it."

"I'd rather drink my coffee," Zak said, and Darby giggled.

"She meant me."

"Ahhh." Zak joined the little girl at the table, then took a notebook from his jacket pocket. "How old are you now Darby?"

"Eight." Her gaze tracked her mother's progress as Patsy carried the promised milk and scone to the table.

"Eight going on eighteen." Patsy placed the milk in front of her daughter, then carefully cut the scone in half.

Zak's mouth watered at the sight of the creamy pastry and the juicy pink bits of fruit. Rather than indulge, he lifted his gaze to the little girl. "What happened at recess?"

"Well, me and my friends were playing on the monkey bars. I climbed right to the top and that was when I saw the man. He was standing by his truck, right next to the playground."

"Had you ever seen this man before? Maybe in town, or

at church?"

Darby shook her head firmly. "He was a stranger."

"Tell me more, Darby. Was he watching you in particular, do you think? Or looking at all the children?"

"I felt like he was staring right at me. Then he waved his hand, like he wanted me to come over."

Patsy compressed her lips and shot Zak a worried glance. Zak kept his attention on Darby.

"What did the man look like?"

"He was old, and he had a beard. And a cowboy hat."

The man Ellie Somers saw had a beard and was wearing a cowboy hat. Could be coincidence. A lot of men in the county fit the same description. "Why do you say he was old?"

"His beard was gray. And his eyes looked tired and droopy. Like Grandpa's."

"You're doing really well, Darby. Tell me about his truck. What color was it?"

Darby shrugged. "I'm not sure. It was a truck, that's all."

"Could you tell if it was clean or dirty?"

She shrugged again. "I didn't really look at it."

"What did you do after the man signaled you to come over?"

"I got creeped out. So I climbed down real fast and told my friends I wanted to play soccer. The field's on the other side of the school, where the man couldn't see us."

"Good for you to get away from him. If you see him

again—or any other person who makes you uncomfortable—you should tell your teacher right away."

"Yeah. That's what my teacher and Mom said. I hope I don't see him again though."

"So do I!" Patsy turned to Zak and he sensed she wanted to ask him more questions, but not in front of her daughter.

"We'll be keeping an eye out for this guy," Zak said, hoping to reassure the both of them. But it wouldn't be easy. The description Darby had provided would fit about 25 percent of the men over fifty in the county. Maybe more. It only took a few weeks to grow a beard, after all. And just five minutes to shave it off.

Chapter Five

NADINE TEXTED ZAK as he was leaving the Snowdrift Café.

Got the warrant. Meet me at the house.

He was there by quarter after five. Daylight hours stretched almost to nine thirty this time of year in Montana and the sun was still well above the protective wall of the Bitterroots. Today Zak was especially grateful for the extra light.

Both Kenny and Nadine's trucks were parked on the street. Nadine was in the process of cordoning off the front yard with crime scene tape.

She moved with purpose and grace, long limbs solid and strong, golden hair tucked up in a bun.

As he got out of his truck, she paused to look at him. He wished he could read the expression in her eyes, but they were concealed by her aviator sunglasses. He resisted the urge to go to her, to touch her. Instead he nodded with professional courtesy and congratulated her on getting the warrant in record time.

"One of my many skills." The quip came out lightly. She

followed it with a frown. "Any theories on what's going on here? Sybil is the last person I'd expect to attract trouble in this town."

"I agree." There were typical reasons a woman of Sybil's age might disappear or be abducted. Money or legal problems. An insanely jealous husband or boyfriend. As far as they knew, Sybil had none of these.

Unless she had secrets. If so, Zak hoped her house would reveal them. They were already running a day behind on this case.

"Kenny here?"

"In the back taking those castings."

Zak nodded at Ellie Somers who watched them from her front window. Then he walked around to the back of the house. From a five-gallon pail, Kenny poured the mixed casting solution around the perimeter of the tire tracks, letting the viscous liquid slowly drain down into the prints he wanted to preserve.

The former mountain guide was taller than Zak, muscular, and fit. Zak had overheard Nadine and Tiff compare Kenny's looks to Bradley Cooper's. Zak didn't care how the guy looked. He was sharp and hardworking and that was what counted.

After years of being put down and bullied by his father and older brothers for being smaller and weaker, Zak had learned to rely on brainpower rather than brawn. But lately he'd learned he had other strengths too. The ability to stay cool in times of crisis. Courage to do the right thing in the face of opposition.

Partly his success at the sheriff's office had developed his sense of self-worth.

And partly the perspective had come with maturity…and his family's departure from Lost Trail to become farmers in South Dakota.

Kenny stopped pouring the liquefied dental stone, raised his head. "Hey, Zak. Anything you want me to do while I wait for this to harden?"

"I could use your help in the house." Zak pulled on a fresh pair of gloves. "I'll open up the house so you and Nadine don't have to crawl in through the window."

As he'd done earlier in the day, Zak removed the screen, raised the window and hoisted his body through the opening. His slender runner's build was a definite asset in this situation.

Once inside he went to the back door. The dead bolt wasn't engaged; all he had to do was twist the doorknob to release the lock. Skirting the broken glass and splattered vegetable juice, he made his way to the foyer. Both the dead bolt and the doorknob lock were engaged at the front door which suggested the potential intruder had used the rear entrance to make his escape.

He undid the locks, then looked around for a key. When they were done here, they'd need to lock up properly. Sybil's purse caught his eye. Carefully he set aside her phone and wallet. Sure enough, her keys were at the bottom of the bag. Two keys and a car fob on one key chain, then, in a separate zipped compartment, a second key chain with two keys. Presumably these would be for the library. Someone would have to check there next.

A few minutes later Kenny came in from the back with the gray plastic case containing their basic evidence collection materials and Nadine entered from the front with the camera bag slung over her shoulder. They gathered in the hallway overlooking the adjoined living and dining areas.

Kenny sat back on his heels and surveyed the place. "Looks like a librarian's house. Lots of books."

This was true. Despite the generous bookshelf in the living room, almost every flat surface had at least one pile of books on it.

"But not a generic librarian. Sybil's personality is all over this place." Nadine pointed out the red, turquoise and yellow cushions on the sofa, a collection of whimsical animal pottery on the fireplace mantel.

Zak thought of Sybil's eyeglasses. She owned several pairs, all in vibrant colors, like those on the cushions. Cheerful colors. Like her personality. He couldn't recall ever seeing her down or despondent.

"Okay, here's the situation. Sybil was last seen yesterday at Natural Grocers, around quarter after six in the evening. We know she made it home because her bag of groceries plus the receipt—with date and time—is on the floor of her foyer, along with her purse and a pair of shoes."

"I saw the purse on my way in," Nadine said. "I take it that was her wallet and cell phone beside it?"

Zak nodded.

"That's not a good sign. No matter how rushed I was, I wouldn't leave home without my wallet and my cell phone." Nadine cocked her head. "Unless there was a fire, or some emergency like that."

Good point. Zak gave Nadine an approving nod. "Even if Sybil did leave the house in a state of panic, for one reason or another, it's been almost twenty-four hours. Time enough for her to let one of her friends or neighbors know she's all right. At the very least she would have wanted someone to tape a note on the library door explaining it wouldn't be open today."

"So where is she?" Kenny asked. "I take it you've already searched the house?"

"Top to bottom." Zak explained how Rosemary Masterson had wondered if Sybil had taken a fall down the basement steps. "Sybil isn't here, but her car is. A neighbor noticed a man in a cowboy hat and beard, driving a dirty pickup truck, turn into her driveway around three yesterday afternoon."

"That why you wanted those castings?" Kenny said.

"Yup. There are signs that a man—for now let's assume the man driving that truck—let himself into Sybil's house through the kitchen—probably using a spare key she kept under a ceramic gnome on her back deck. He used the toilet, completed a crossword puzzle, perhaps poured himself a glass of vegetable cocktail, so I'm guessing he was waiting here for her when she got home."

"Maybe he was someone she knew?" Kenny said.

"It's definitely possible," Zak agreed. "The broken glass and spilled liquid on the kitchen floor, however, suggest someone was startled. Again, not necessarily proof of a crime. But when we take the facts together—Sybil not showing up for work or contacting any friends or neighbors; her keys, wallet and phone still in the house; the missing spare key to her house—I think we have to assume she was removed from her house against her will."

"But who would do that and why?" Nadine asked. "It doesn't make any sense."

"We don't have time to worry about motive right now. Sybil's life may well depend on us finding her as soon as possible. If this guy took her last night around six, he's got almost a day on us." Zak dusted his hands in a 'let's get moving' gesture. "Nadine, you want to take the photos?"

"You bet." She unzipped the case and pulled out the Canon DLSR.

"Make sure you get a clear image of the partial footprint in the spilled liquid on the kitchen floor. Kenny, when she's done in the kitchen, I'd like you to bag the crossword puzzle, the orange peel, the pen, and the shattered glass on the floor. Then see if you can lift any prints from the toilet, the juice box and the fridge."

"You think whoever took Sybil broke the glass?" Kenny asked.

"At first I thought she dropped the glass when the intruder startled her. But this crossword puzzle, and the fact that the toilet seat is up in the bathroom, has me thinking the intruder was here first, and was waiting for her. Could be he dropped the glass when he grabbed her. I'm open to other theories."

Nadine and Kenny exchanged glances but didn't share any alternate thoughts. Maybe they'd have some later.

Zak went to the study, anxious to get a look at Sybil's laptop. So many people were surprisingly careless with their computers, not only leaving them on but with windows open showing Facebook pages and email accounts, internet searches, and some even left written lists of passcodes in plain sight.

Sybil's office was in the small room intended as a second bedroom. Despite the limited square footage, she'd managed to squeeze in a large desk and credenza as well as an armchair covered in a colorful floral pattern, and an exercise bike.

The seat of the bike was dusty, but the chair looked well used, the indent of Sybil's plump body outlined in the soft cushions.

On the wall were colorful, sensual prints of flowers. Zak wasn't an art expert, but even a novice like him recognized Georgia O'Keeffe's work.

Zak sat at the desk amid piles of books, most of them new releases, though a few looked like well-thumbed classics. A red ceramic mug held a collection of pens and pencils and next to that was an old-fashioned Day-Timer.

He turned to the laptop, opening it gently.

Sybil turned out to be one of those computer users who wasn't as careful as she should have been, because as soon as Zak touched her keyboard the screen lit up…with Sybil's profile page on a dating site. Whoa!

Only a pornography site would have startled Zak more. He stared at the screen as his brain processed the fact that Sybil had been in search of romance, sex, or some combination of the two.

He realized he'd been blindsided by his youth into the mistaken assumption that a woman of Sybil's age wouldn't be interested in these things. Those sensuous painting of flowers should have been his first clue.

He pushed aside the automatic guilt he felt at invading Sybil's privacy and studied her home page. There were unread messages from three men. Two of them were dated early in April. The third was more recent…only a few hours ago.

Zak clicked on the most recent message. The site informed him the session had timed out and he needed to log in again. This turned out to be no problem because the computer handily offered him Sybil's username and password automatically.

Oh, Sybil. If he found her, he was going to lecture her on computer security.

When he found her.

"How are things going in here?"

Nadine's voice jerked him back to the present. She leaned against the doorframe, head tilted as she waited for his response.

He didn't keep her in suspense. "Guess who was active on Montana Matches?"

"You're kidding." Nadine hurried forward and peered over his shoulder. "Oh my God. Sybil had three matches."

"I don't think she was interested in these two—Zane and Martin. They both sent her messages back in April that she never bothered to read, let alone answer."

Zak moved the cursor over a photo of a man with glasses and a neat goatee. "There's a long chain of messages between her and this third guy though—Jeffery Taylor, a high school principal from Missoula—including two from last night and three from today that she never opened."

"Could he be the dude in the truck Ellie saw yesterday?"

"Ellie said he had a beard. Not sure if Jeffery Taylor's goatee would qualify." Zak clicked on the photos of the other two men. Zane, a retired professor from the University of Montana, had a full beard. Martin, a sales rep also from Missoula, was the only clean-shaven one, but that didn't necessarily mean he hadn't subsequently grown a beard.

"Let me see if I can print off photos so we can show

them to Ellie." Zak examined the cables at the side of the laptop. One was for power. The other led to a printer on a ledge under the desk. "We're in luck. Sybil's got a color printer."

He checked to make sure there was enough paper in the tray, then began selecting pages to print. He wanted not only the photographs of the men but also copies of the conversations they'd had with Sybil.

Nadine leaned closer to the screen, bringing with her the scent of coconut shampoo. "Sybil joined the site in mid-March. She calls herself 'an intelligent woman who enjoys conversations about books and ideas, quiet dinners and playing chess and word games.'"

"Not the sort of description you'd expect to attract a predator."

Yet maybe it had. An hour ago Zak had no idea who might have abducted Sybil. Now he had three persons of interest to investigate.

NADINE FELT LIKE an intruder, unlocking the front door of the library. She'd never been in here without Sybil. But Zak had sent her over to do a preliminary investigation, giving the polite request—which was really an order—in the same tone he'd used when asking Kenny to keep working at the house, to make sure they hadn't missed anything.

Zak was so adept at switching from professional boss to warm-and-caring boyfriend, she couldn't tell which role he preferred. But this was no time to ponder the viability of their relationship. The first days of an abduction case were crucial, and with only the three of them, they were spread thin.

Converted from a two-story home, the library had a cozy and welcoming vibe. Full credit to Sybil who ran the place with the help of a half dozen volunteers.

There were buckets of pussy willows and forsythia blossoms on the front porch, dozens of pairs of hand-knitted slippers in a basket at the entry, and an intriguing collection of books focused on Montana—the national parks, the ranching and copper-mining history, some poetry volumes and mysteries from local authors—on a table in the room to the left of the foyer.

In the next room—the home's former dining area—was the non-fiction section. Sybil's desk was here, angled so she could see not only the entire room, but also the foyer.

Nadine would come back to this desk, but first she needed to do a security check.

The thud of her boots on the wooden floors sounded inordinately loud in the oppressively silent library. Nadine checked every room on both levels. The stacks of books and homey reading areas were all neat and tidy. She saw no broken windows or other signs of forced entry or struggle. In the back room on the second level were two long tables with several computers for patrons to use.

Nadine inspected each one. They were all powered off.

In the fiction section she paused at the shelf with all the romances. How many of these had Amber read? Nadine could imagine the young woman curled up in the armchair by the window, lost in a fantasy world where mothers never died, and fathers were strong and supportive, not moody and angry.

The question was, did Amber's father do more than lose his temper? Did he hurt Amber physically as well?

Nadine vowed to check on the young woman as soon as she could. Tuesday or Wednesday at the latest. Hopefully Sybil would be found by then, unharmed, the mystery of her disappearance resolved.

On that happy thought, Nadine returned to Sybil's desk, slipping on a pair of gloves before tapping on the computer keyboard. Not so lucky here as Zak had been in the house. Sybil had powered down the computer at the end of the day. Nadine glanced around for a potential source for the password.

The desk surface was covered with piles of books and papers, a collection of plastic Smurf figurines, and a ceramic mug half-full of scummy-looking coffee. A lined notepad on the right-hand side of the desk contained a running to-do list. About a third of the items were crossed off. Nadine flipped through the pad. No passwords anywhere.

She examined the to-do list again, skimming over the

work-related items. Her attention was snagged when she saw: *Order more books for Amber.* She smiled at: *Clean floor cushion Ryan peed on.* And tensed at: *Show letter to Sheriff?*

What letter? Nadine's adrenaline surged. It wasn't on the desktop. Maybe in the drawers? She rifled through the top desk drawer. Nothing, just stationery supplies, a bag of mints, a half-dozen eyeglass cases.

The second drawer. Random papers.

The last drawer had a stack of library periodicals and tucked down the side…a business-sized envelope, one end ripped off.

She pulled it out and studied it. There was no return address, but the postal stamp was Missoula.

Inside was a single sheet of paper.

Gloves sticking, she pulled out the sheet of paper.

I want a second chance. You owe me.

Chapter Six

"I HAD NO idea Sybil was dating men she met online."

Rosemary Masterson looked as if Zak had just told her Sybil ran a prostitution ring out of the library. She lowered her gaze to her hands, adjusted her engagement and wedding bands just so.

"Although, now that I think of it, Sybil did mention the Montana Match dating site to me a few months ago. I thought she meant it for me. That I should start dating again. I shot the idea down immediately, of course."

"Why do you say *of course*?" Tiff asked.

They were in the kitchen at Raven Farm. Zak had been a guest in this house many times, but this was the first time he could remember Tiff, not her mother, acting the hostess. She'd already poured them all coffee. Now she set out a plate of ginger cookies.

Her mother, fine-featured like her daughter, slumped in a chair at the table. In front of her lay a piece of paper containing a long list of Sybil's friends and neighbors.

"Do you mean you're against online dating sites? Or dating in general?" Tiff pressed her mother for an answer.

"Dating in general. I'm too old."

"Not true, Mom."

Zak agreed with Tiff, but they had more important subjects to discuss right now.

He picked up the paper with the list of names. A small 'x' had been placed next to each. "Have you phoned everyone here?"

"We have." Rosemary gave a disheartened shrug. "Everyone is as clueless as I am. We can't think where Sybil might have gone. No one can name anyone who might have wished her harm."

Zak was disappointed but not surprised. "I know Sybil's parents died a while ago and she didn't have siblings. Is there any other family we could call?"

"Afraid not. Sybil had one aunt and uncle somewhere in Georgia. But I believe they've passed on too." Rosemary half-lifted her coffee, then set the mug down again. "Something bad must have happened to her. I can count on one hand the number of days she hasn't opened the library. And she would never cause this much worry intentionally."

"I agree," Tiff said, her voice grave. "At the same time, it's so difficult to imagine anyone wanting to hurt her."

"She ever talk about money problems? Being financially strapped?"

"Her only money problem was how to invest her savings," Tiff said. "She asked me for some investment advice in March. She's not rich, but she has ample savings, plus she owns her own house."

So much for that angle.

"What about men?" Zak turned back to Rosemary. If anyone would have the inside scoop on the men Sybil had been dating, it had to be her best friend.

His initial review of the messages Sybil had exchanged with the three men on the dating site hadn't exposed any dangerous signals. Martin and Zane sounded disappointed when Sybil informed them after their first coffee date that she didn't want to see them again. But though both had tried to get her to change her mind, neither had seemed unhinged by the rejection.

As for Jeffery, his online conversations with Sybil seemed the normal sort of banter between a man and a woman looking to get to know one another.

But maybe one of them had said something to Sybil in person. Something she'd shared with Rosemary…

Zak took out the photographs of the three men from the dating site. Earlier he'd showed them to Ellie Somers, hoping she'd recognize the driver of the truck. She'd studied them for a long time, but in the end hadn't been able to give him a conclusive answer. She'd confessed that, even with her glasses on, she didn't see so well these days.

It might be a truthful answer, but it sure wasn't helpful.

"Did Sybil ever mention any of these men to you?" Zak spread the three photographs on the table. He'd printed their names on the bottom of each piece of paper and now he read them aloud.

"Jeffery Taylor," he pointed to the man with the goatee and glasses, "is a principal at a high school in Missoula."

Next, he indicated the man with the salt-and-pepper beard. "Dr. Zane Elser is a retired history professor."

Finally he pushed forward the photo of the clean-shaven man wearing the shirt and tie. "This is Martin Thomson. He's a sales rep."

Rosemary shifted the pictures around the table like they were puzzle pieces, focusing on first one, then the second, and the third. "I've never seen any of these men before. Sybil certainly didn't mention them to me."

So much for that hope. "Do you know of any other men Sybil dated in her past?"

"Not really. No."

"What about when she was younger?"

"In high school and college she dated quite a bit, but there was no one special."

"You went to college in Missoula together, didn't you?"

"We did. After my degree I came home. Sybil moved to Boston for her postgrad work. We lost contact in those years. I was busy getting married, having my first baby."

Rosemary frowned here, no doubt thinking of how her doctor and her sister had conspired to switch her healthy son for an infant with a congenital heart defect. Casey had died when he was just twelve years old.

Justin Pittman, however, was still alive. All of them—

Rosemary, Tiff and Justin—were still coming to terms with the fact that they were related.

"When did Sybil move back to Lost Trail?"

"Must have been around the age of twenty-six or twenty-seven. Her parents and friends—me included—were pleased, but surprised. Sybil was so smart, so academic. We all thought she'd have a career in Seattle or Portland. And then she shocked us all with her plan to open a library in our little town."

"She made good on that plan," Zak said. And he was thankful. He couldn't imagine surviving his childhood without the library. Sybil had been a guiding hand in his intellectual development for as long as he could remember. "But if she moved back here in her twenties, doesn't it seem odd she never had any romantic relationships in all that time?"

"I guess." Rosemary started playing with her rings again. "Sybil told me she preferred living alone. Maybe I should have probed a little more, but I was too preoccupied with my own problems. I guess I wasn't as good of a friend to her as I should have been."

Rosemary turned her head to the side, wiped a tear from her eye. "She was always here for me. When Casey died, then Irving, and my sister. She was such a good friend. And I took it all for granted."

Tiff covered her mother's hands with her own. "You've had an extraordinarily difficult life, Mom. Don't beat yourself up for not being there for Sybil. If she didn't talk about her love life, she probably had her reasons."

✕

TIFF WASN'T SURPRISED when Kenny called to cancel their date at the Dew Drop Inn, shortly after Zak left. She understood the need for the sheriff's team to work quickly, to make Sybil's disappearance a priority.

Anyway, she couldn't leave her mother alone. Book club had been canceled when it became clear Sybil wasn't going to show up. Now her mom was pacing the kitchen floor, wringing her hands.

"I just pray Sybil's okay. You don't think she could be...?" Rosemary couldn't finish the sentence.

Tiff topped up their wine. Her mother rarely had more than one glass. Tonight was going to be an exception. "Zak was talking like he expected to find her alive and unharmed. We have to believe he will. Otherwise we'll go crazy."

"Yes." Rosemary carried her glass with her as she paced to the eating area on the far side of the kitchen. She gazed out the window, over the fields of fir and spruce and pine trees, to the pink glow over the Bitterroots where the sun had just set.

Tiff thought of other times she and her mother had sat and worried about someone they loved. Most recently it had been for her brother, Justin, during his fight with cancer.

Her mom must have been thinking on the same lines because she said, “I’d like to call Justin. Do you think it’s too late?”

“It’s only nine thirty. Where’s your cell phone?”

“By the sink in the kitchen.”

While Tiff went to retrieve it, her mother kept talking.

“Before I phone Justin, there’s something I should talk to you about.” Her mother took a long swallow of wine, then squared her shoulders. “I’m thinking of discontinuing our Sunday family dinners.”

“But I thought you loved those dinners?” They had been her mother’s idea, back when she’d first discovered Justin Pittman—who’d been raised by the town’s doctor, Clark Pittman—was her biological son. Rosemary had wanted to forge a familial bond with her adult son, and this included embracing Justin’s adopted daughter Geneva and even the man he thought of as his father.

The inclusion of Clark had been particularly generous since the doctor had known about the baby switching and done nothing to stop it. But her mother, who’d lost Casey, the boy she’d raised and loved as her son, as well as her husband and her sister, had claimed to want to forgive and move on.

“I love spending time with Justin and Geneva. But I’m finding it harder and harder to be around Clark.”

Tiff let out a long sigh. So this was what her mother had been stressed about. What a relief. “I always wondered how you could be so forgiving."

"I think I was in shock. And then we found out Justin was sick. All that mattered was getting him well again."

"Which he finally is."

"Thank God." Her mother swirled the wine in her glass and took another deep breath. "Do you think Clark's role in switching Casey and Justin was as passive as he made it out to be?"

"I suspect it wasn't. He was the doctor, after all. The one in charge." It felt great to finally say the words aloud. For a long time Tiff had struggled to repress her anger about the crime. She'd figured if her mother could forgive, so should she. After all, her loss of a brother was not on par with her mother's loss of a son.

But despite Tiff's best efforts, a black pool of anger and resentment had simmered inside her. Sometimes she could hardly stand to look at Clark, let alone speak to him.

Finally she could share her secret thoughts with her mom. "Aunt Marsha never left a suicide note. The only version of the truth we've heard was from Clark."

"And he was so careful to pin all the blame on my sister. While he painted himself as a devoted husband who loved his wife too much to let her know her baby had been born with a serious heart defect." Rosemary leaned her head against the wall, as if the burden of all her losses was getting to be too heavy.

They would never know the full truth of what had happened that night, or of the evil pact between Marsha and Clark. But one thing was certain, Clark's penance—closing his clinic, retiring as a doctor—had been a pittance compared with his crime.

"We could still get Clark arrested. Do you want me to talk to Zak?"

Rosemary was silent for a while. Finally she sighed. "Maybe. Once Sybil's been found, and we know she's okay. In the meantime, I'll just talk to Justin and let him know what I've decided. Clark Pittman is no longer welcome in this house."

Chapter Seven

ZAK HAD MISSED a call from Nadine while he was at Raven Farm talking to Rosemary and Tiff. On his drive back to the office, he returned it.

"What's up? Where are you?"

"Home. I had to do the chores."

Referencing Nadine's chores was their private joke. It made her sound like a real rancher when all she had on her acreage so far was her horse, Making Magic, and her dog, Junior.

"I found something in Sybil's desk at the library," Nadine continued.

Zak's shoulders tensed. He was already back in town, cruising along Tumbleweed Road, about to turn onto Main. The western sky was awash in violets and pinks, a reminder that the first day of their investigation was about to end. "Tell me."

"An anonymous letter. I left it on your desk. It was postmarked in Missoula. Just two sentences: *I want a second chance. You owe me.*"

"That sounds stalkerish."

"Agreed."

"Could you see the date on the postmark?"

"It was blurry. But Sybil kept a to-do list on her desk and the last item on it was '*Show letter to Sheriff.*' So, I'm betting she received the letter on Thursday, her last day at work."

"I wish she had told me. Right away."

"Hindsight, right?"

As he turned onto Main, he noticed Gertie Humphrey from the gas station convenience store, her short bony legs working hard to keep up with the dog on the end of her leash. Since when did Gertie have a dog?

"Was the note printed off a computer?" he asked, coming back to their conversation.

"Handwritten. And before you ask, I compared it to the printing in the crossword puzzle. I'm no expert but the two samples look similar to me."

"Huh. Good work, Nadine."

He paused, wanting to shift the conversation from work to personal, but not sure what to say. He'd be working late tonight. She probably didn't want him crawling into her bed in the wee hours of the night.

So he just said good night. A moment later he pulled into his parking space behind the two-story brick building that housed the Lost Trail Sheriff's Office. He bounded up the stairs to the second level. Bea had finally gone home, but Kenny was at his desk.

The deputy waved at the coffee machine. "Just made a

fresh pot. Also ordered some pizza. Help yourself."

"Good man." Zak grabbed a slice of the pepperoni and mushroom pie. For a few minutes they chatted, catching up on each other's progress.

Kenny had bagged Sybil's phone, as well as the other evidence Zak had requested. He passed the phone to Zak. "That Jeffery Taylor has been trying to reach Sybil since yesterday evening. Could be genuine concern, could be his way of covering tracks."

Zak nodded as he scrolled through the list of missed calls. Lots from Rosemary Masterson, others from Debbie-Ann, Ellie Somers, and a few names he recognized from the list of book club members Rosemary had given him.

Of all the callers, Jeffery Taylor was the only male. "I'll call Taylor now and set up a meeting for tomorrow morning."

"Want me to call the other dudes she met on that dating site?"

"That would be great. See if you can set up meetings for tomorrow. Hopefully they all live in the Missoula area." Didn't matter tomorrow was Saturday. Weekends and preorganized schedules had no meaning at a time like this. "We'll need to start running background checks on these guys as well."

"Count me in."

Zak turned at the sound of Nadine's voice. She was at the doorway, dressed in civilian clothes, jeans and a gray sweatshirt. As she stepped forward, he caught the faint scent of hay layered over coconut shampoo. Her signature scent.

"You're back."

"Chores done, I'm ready to work." She registered the surprise on Zak's face. "What? You didn't think I was going to bail on you guys, did you?"

IT HAD BEEN dark for an hour, the pizza box was empty, the coffeepot down to the dregs, when Zak called Kenny and Nadine into his office to compare notes. He came out from behind his desk and joined them at the table he'd moved into the corner of the room. Sheriff Ford had preferred barking orders from behind his desk. Regular staff meetings, at this new table, were one of the first changes Zak made once he took charge.

First Zak caught Nadine and Kenny up with Darby Larkin's complaint about an older man trying to lure her off the playground at recess. "Probably not related to Sybil's disappearance, but you never know. We'll need to do extra patrols around the school for the next while to keep an eye on the situation. Nadine, did you tell Kenny about the note you found in Sybil's desk at the library?"

She nodded. "We've got it bagged for evidence and I've made a copy for the files."

"Okay, then, moving on to our persons of interest in

Sybil's disappearance...Jeffery Taylor checks out fine so far. He's a principal at Rocky High School in Missoula. Been widowed two years, no children. His online conversations with Sybil were mostly about books and movies. Intellectual. Nothing too personal. I called him at home, and he said he's been worried about Sybil since he couldn't reach her Thursday evening. They had plans to attend an afternoon concert in Missoula on Sunday. I'm going to meet up with him at his home tomorrow. He sounded genuinely concerned and anxious to help."

"O-kay." Nadine's tone was skeptical. "He sounds almost too squeaky clean to me."

"We'll know more once we've interviewed him," Zak agreed. "Kenny, what about guy number two?"

"Martin is a bit more interesting." Kenny referenced his phone where he kept all his notes. "Thomson has two ex-wives, four children, and works as a sales rep for Secure Zone." Kenny looked up from the phone. "That's a company that sells payment processing systems."

Zak nodded. He'd heard of it.

"Martin is on the road a lot. Seems to spend a fair amount of time online in the evenings. He's made contact with dozens of women on Montana Match. The majority seem to lose interest after their first 'in person' meeting."

"Like Sybil," Nadine said. "I wonder how Martin felt about all that rejection? You think maybe he reached a breaking point?"

"That's possible," Zak agreed. "Did you get to talk to the man, Kenny?"

"Yeah. He's in Bozeman, won't be coming back to Missoula for another two weeks. When I asked him about Sybil, he said he hadn't heard from her in over a month. He did sound bitter about that."

"That timing is consistent with the messages on the dating site. Tomorrow how about you call the department in Bozeman and see if they'll send someone to check on his whereabouts Thursday night? See if we can get some corroboration on his location."

"Will do."

Kenny made a note on his phone. The guy almost never used pen and paper, while Zak preferred to keep written notes on the job. Old-school.

"How about our number three man, Nadine? What did you find out about Dr. Zane Elser?"

Nadine set a stack of papers on the table, flipped through them, then pulled one to the top. "Zane Elser is a retired history professor from UM. He's never been married and—here's where it gets interesting—he's active on at least five dating sites, using the same profile name. Montana Matches seems to be the only one where he connects with women his own age. On the other sites he lists his age as thirty-five and uses a much younger photo of himself."

"How can he get away with that?" Kenny asked. "As soon as the women meet him, they'll know the truth."

"Unless he didn't actually meet the younger women," Zak speculated. "Maybe he was just after some titillating conversation."

"I've saved the best for last," Nadine said. "The year Elser retired he was charged with sexual assault for inappropriate advances by one of his students. The charges were later dropped due to insufficient evidence."

"The guy sure sounds like a perv," Kenny said. "But if he likes younger women…does it follow he'd abduct someone like Sybil?"

"He used his regular age on Montana Matches," Nadine reminded them. "So, he wasn't exclusively into younger women."

"Zane Elser is definitely worth a follow-up," Zak said.

"Which will be easier to do than you think. He lives by himself on a ten-acre plot of land west of Big Hole Road."

"That makes him practically a neighbor." Big Hole Road ran the eastern border of their county, in the middle of a whole bunch of nothing. "Wonder why he moved from Missoula to such a remote location?"

"Maybe the guy is antisocial," Kenny said.

"Or maybe he's got secrets he wants to protect." Zak turned back to Nadine. "Did you get in touch with him and set up a meeting?"

"No. When I saw where he lived, I figured it might be smart for us to show up unannounced."

Zak nodded slowly. "Catch him with his guard down. I

like that. Kenny, how about you handle the meeting with Jeffery Taylor in Missoula tomorrow? Nadine and I will drive out to Shirley's Peak and pay a surprise visit to our history prof."

Chapter Eight

"I NEVER THOUGHT I would feel afraid in Lost Trail. But I am afraid. I could not cope if something happened to Ashley."

Though his girlfriend, Debbie-Ann, was speaking the words, Justin Pittman, felt the same fear. He'd come to parenting late, when Geneva was already four, but she'd quickly become the most important thing in his life.

He turned off the TV and dimmed the bedroom lights, while Debbie-Ann drew a blanket over their daughters. They'd fallen asleep in Justin's bed, while watching *Zootopia*. Despite an age gap of several years, they were great friends, Debbie-Ann's platinum-haired, ballet-loving Ashley and his raven-haired, tiny Geneva, with the café au lait skin she'd inherited from her mother.

He waited as Debbie-Ann dropped soft kisses on both girls' cheeks.

"Another glass of wine?" he offered.

Debbie-Ann nodded and followed him to the kitchen. Finally they could talk freely about the day's disturbing events without fear of the kids overhearing.

"We need to watch them carefully, make sure they're never alone, not even for a minute. I wonder if I should hire extra staff at the day care?"

"I agree we should take precautions. I'm not sure we need to panic." He filled two glasses with the malbec left over from dinner and passed one to Debbie-Ann. "What did Patsy say exactly?"

The owner of the Snowdrift Café had called while he and Debbie-Ann were cleaning up after dinner. Justin had heard just one side of the conversation.

"During recess today, an older man tried to lure Darby off the playground. Doesn't that sound panic-worthy?"

"Did the man talk to Darby?"

"Apparently he gestured for her to come closer. Darby ran in the opposite direction."

"Smart girl." Justin's lawyerly brain required more facts. "Did anyone else see this guy?"

"Unfortunately not. And Darby's description is vague. An older man with a beard wearing a cowboy hat." Debbie-Ann shrugged. "Know anyone matching that description in town?"

He let one side of his mouth curl up. There were so many. But… "It sounds like the description Ellie Somers gave of the man she saw driving up to Sybil's house yesterday." This was the second subject he and Debbie-Ann hadn't had a chance to discuss.

Debbie-Ann's eyes zoomed in on him. "I'm so worried

about Sybil I can't stand it. Do you think she's okay?"

"We have to hope she is. You can bet Zak and his team are working around the clock to find her."

"There is way too much crazy stuff happening in our town. You think that guy who tried to abduct Darby also took Sybil?"

"Most of the sick perverts who abduct women or children, go after a certain 'type' of victim," Justin pointed out. "Some guys like redheads, some like children. But we're getting ahead of ourselves. We don't know that man intended to abduct Darby. And we don't know that Sybil was abducted either."

Debbie-Ann sank into one of the kitchen chairs, shoulders slumped, mouth drawn. "No, we don't know. But it's possible. We may have *two* dangerous predators to worry about."

Justin shook his head wearily. "That defies the laws of probability, doesn't it?"

Debbie-Ann shivered, wrapped her arms around her torso. "I've lived in Lost Trail all my life. I have no problem sleeping with my window open in the summer. Half the time I even forget to lock my front door. But for the first time ever, I'm afraid to go home. I'm terrified I'll fall asleep and when I wake up Ashley won't be in her bed."

"Stay the night." Justin touched her shoulder, stroked his fingers over the knotted muscles that led to her neck. "The kids are already asleep."

Because it was the weekend, or maybe because of her fear, Debbie-Ann had stayed later than usual and now it was almost ten. Truth was, he'd sleep better knowing she and Ashley were safe under his roof.

Debbie-Ann leaned her head into his hand. "I'd like that. But I'm not sure it would be sending the right message to the children."

"That all depends on what message we want to send them." He pulled a chair right up in front of her and straddled it. With his hands he cupped her face. Debbie-Ann did not take much stock in her looks. She trimmed her own hair, wore very little makeup, never bothered with jewelry. But he had never known a woman with a warmer smile or kinder eyes.

They'd started as friends, single parents who banded together to help one another through the rough patches. Over time their feelings had shifted. They didn't get much alone time, but six months ago he'd asked her on a proper date. Within weeks, they'd become lovers. The progression had felt as natural to Justin as becoming a father had been.

"I love you, Debbie-Ann." He'd never stated the words out loud before, though in a hundred actions and looks they'd been implied.

"Do you? Sometimes I worry…well, there aren't a lot of dating options for either of us in this town."

"Is that why you're with me?"

"No. Of course not."

"Me either. I do love you. I'm not sure why it took me so long to tell you."

"I have a hunch." Debbie-Ann ran her fingers through his hair. She did that a lot since it had grown back. "It's because of Willow."

He couldn't deny it was true. "I married her for all the wrong reasons. I want to get it right this time."

"And is it? Right this time?"

"For me it is." At the end of each day, this was the woman he wanted to see. He was drawn to her sweet, caring nature, her subtle wit and sense of humor. Most of all her stability and sanity—qualities in which his first wife, Geneva's mother Willow—had been decidedly deficient.

Gazing into the honey and whiskey warmth of Debbie-Ann's eyes, the urge to make a marriage proposal had never been stronger. But not before he'd told her the entire truth about his parents.

"Just stay," he urged her. "Let me hold you tonight and make you feel safe. I promise the kids will handle it fine in the morning." He knew for certain Geneva would be delighted. She was always saying how lucky Ashley was to have such a nice mom.

"Okay, I'll stay."

To his relief, a smile had replaced her worry lines.

She leaned forward until their noses were touching. "And for the record...I love you too."

"I was wondering if you were going to admit it. I do recall you once saying I was too old for you."

"True. But I've decided to relax my standards." She kissed him briefly, then pulled back. "It's been a long day. Mind if I take a shower before bed?"

"Make yourself at home." She knew where he kept his extra towels and toiletries.

Ten minutes later, while she was still in the bathroom, his doorbell rang. Adrenaline hit him like an electrical shot. Instantly he mocked himself for overreacting. Bad guys didn't generally ring doorbells.

The family dog, Dora, was already at the front door, tail wagging like an overactive windshield wiper. Justin shot a look out the front window…and was surprised to see his father on the stoop.

He hurried to open the door. "Dad…are you okay?"

Justin's feelings about the man who had raised him were complicated. There was love, but also resentment, and even anger. Underlying all of these was a sense of obligation. As he aged, his father was becoming more dependent on Justin. Their usual pattern was to have lunch once a week and to share Sunday dinners. But ironically as Justin had grown stronger in the year since his stem-cell transplant, his father had become weaker. Lately Clark had begun phoning Justin several times a day, becoming almost clingy.

Clark had lost his interest in discussing current affairs, in reading the daily papers and going to church on Sundays. Instead, he lingered in bed most mornings and spent afternoons in long, aimless drives in the vast countryside.

Once a fastidious man who had strong opinions on how to iron a shirt, and the importance of matching the color of his belt to his shoes, Clark had stopped shaving regularly and often left the house wearing sweatpants and T-shirts—clothing Justin hadn't even known his father owned.

Geneva had noticed the changes too and had started avoiding spending time with her gramps. It made Justin sad, but his dad didn't even seem to care. It was as if Justin was the only person who mattered to him now. Even during Sunday family dinners at Raven Farm, his father rarely spoke to anyone but him.

"I'm fine, Justin. I just need to talk to you. I have a wonderful idea!"

As recently as six months ago, his father would never have dreamed of showing up this late, unannounced, no matter how 'wonderful' the idea.

"That sounds interesting, Dad. Why don't we meet for lunch tomorrow and you can tell me all about it?" He leaned in close and took a good sniff, just to make sure his dad hadn't been drinking. All he could smell was coffee. "Have you eaten today, Dad?"

His father stuck a finger in his ear, rubbed it this way and that, as if trying to improve his hearing. "Food? I had a sandwich. I think."

That was another problem. His father no longer ate regular meals and the weight was dropping off.

He really didn't want to invite his father in, but if he sent him home now, who knew when he would eat again. Justin put his arm around his father's frail shoulders and led him to the kitchen.

"How'd you like some roast chicken and potatoes? I'll heat it up for you."

His father sat quietly while Justin dished out the food then set the plate in the microwave to heat. Along with the meal, he gave his father a glass of milk.

"Smells great," Clark said, when Justin set the plate in front of him. But he only picked at the food, seeming more interested in looking around. "Have you ever thought that with Geneva getting older, you might be outgrowing this place?"

"We're fine."

Suddenly the background noise of running water stopped. His father cocked his head at the ensuing silence.

"Is that Geneva in the bathroom? Isn't it late for her to be up?"

"It's Debbie-Ann. She and Ashley are staying the night."

That news earned him a scowl.

"That's not smart, Son. People will talk, you know. Get the wrong idea."

"Or maybe they'll get the right idea. Debbie-Ann and I, we're getting serious."

The fork clattered to the table. Clark shook his head. "What are you talking about? You and Debbie-Ann are just friends."

"That's how we started." He hadn't expected this news to be either upsetting or startling. Surely his father had noticed how important Debbie-Ann and Ashley were to him. "Hey, what was that idea you wanted to tell me about?"

His father frowned. His eyes shifted in confusion. And then he gave a small nod. "Yes. My idea. Geneva's getting bigger and this house is too small. You and Geneva should move in with me."

A movement from the hallway caught his eye. Debbie-Ann was there, wrapped up in his terry towel robe, wet hair dripping. Before he could acknowledge her presence, she slipped out of view.

Justin turned back to his father. So this was life in the sandwich generation. What the hell was he supposed to say?

Chapter Nine

IT WAS PAST midnight and Zak was still at his desk, working on reports. A lot had happened today, which meant there was a ton of documentation to be completed. When Ford had been sheriff, Zak had done most of this work for him. But Zak didn't expect—or want—any of his employees doing his paperwork. Often the process of thinking through the day, writing out the details, helped clarify his thinking.

Little details that may have been glossed over during the rush of activity would come to the surface.

Like the one he'd noticed in the crime scene photos the third time he examined them. He couldn't believe he hadn't focused on it earlier.

He stepped out to the main office. Kenny and Nadine were still at their desks, processing evidence and writing their own reports, handling the countless administrative duties that always trailed an active investigation.

The pizza was gone. The coffeepot empty. They were all running on nerves and determination.

"The teddy bear."

His deputies looked up, eyes bleary, expressions flat.

Then Nadine's eyebrows arched. "The one on Sybil's kitchen counter?"

"Yes. Did that strike you as odd?"

"Not overly. Some adult women are into stuffed animals. I have a friend who displays the Beanie Babies she had as a child."

"And my grandmother has two stuffed monkeys she keeps on her bed," Kenny added. "They were a Valentine's Day gift from my grandfather."

"Okay." Zak had to accept such behavior was normal. In the house where he'd grown up stuffed animals had not played any role, whatsoever. "Let's say the bear had some sort of sentimental value. Doesn't the kitchen counter seem like an odd place to keep it?"

Nadine and Kenny exchanged a glance that suggested he was overreaching.

Maybe the teddy bear hadn't been such a key insight after all.

Kenny yawned, stretched out his muscular arms. "I can't think straight anymore. Need sleep."

"Good idea." Zak looked at Nadine. She was rubbing her fingers over her left eyebrow, something she did when stressed or tired.

"Want me to drop our evidence off at the lab when I'm in Missoula tomorrow?" Kenny offered.

"Excellent idea," Zak agreed, his gaze still on Nadine.

She'd started to tidy her desk in slow, deliberate movements. Probably too tired to move any faster.

Kenny took the evidence bags from his desk to the lock-up. "I plan to be on the road at dawn. I'll be in touch after my meeting with Jeffery Taylor."

"Thanks," Zak said.

A moment later, Kenny was gone. Here was his opportunity to have a private word with Nadine. He couldn't tell from her expression what she was feeling right now, other than exhaustion.

"It's been a hell of a day," he said. "And it won't be getting better until we find Sybil."

"I hope we find her soon. I hate to think what she might be going through right now." Nadine stared out the window, just as he'd done earlier, as if hoping to see some clue of the missing librarian's location.

"Don't beat yourself up with those kinds of thoughts. Stay focused on the investigation." He took one of Nadine's hands. Linked their fingers. "This sheriff thing. It seemed like a good idea last year when I decided to run. But it's pretty much consuming all my time."

"Really? I hadn't noticed." Nadine's laugh sounded forced. Then she shook her head. "I'm glad you ran. This town needed a shake-up. And you were the right man."

But was he the right man for her? Maybe he lacked the courage or maybe he was just too damn tired, but he couldn't ask the question tonight.

"I would have stepped aside if you wanted to run." He didn't say the words lightly. He meant them.

"I'm glad I didn't. I don't want my job to be my entire life. I need time for my horse, and my dog, and for...other things."

"I want...others thing, too."

"Yeah? Such as?"

He took her other hand, too. Pulled her in closer. "More time for you."

"So you think this working together and you being my boss...it's not a problem?"

"Not as far as I'm concerned." He drew back a little. "Is it for you?"

"Not now. But what about the future? I mean, if we stay together. If we..."

He waited, hoping she would suggest moving in together. He was so ready for that step. But he felt awkward bringing up the subject. She owned an acreage; he lived in a basement suite. Obviously it was her home they'd move into. So the initiative ought to come from her.

When it was clear she was waiting for him to speak, he decided to punt. "Let's not worry about the future right now. We have lots of time."

Nadine dropped her gaze. He sensed he'd said the wrong thing. "Maybe this is just a short-term problem. Next term I might not get reelected."

"Don't even say that! This is the perfect job for you."

He couldn't deny it. From the start his role as sheriff had felt like a broken-in pair of running shoes. An extension of himself.

"Yeah, I love it. But this working seven days a week—it can't go on. Once I wrangle our budget into shape and find us money for a new deputy…"

He stopped. In all honesty he couldn't see hiring anyone new for at least another year. He sighed, shoulders slumping at the reality.

She let go of his hands. "You'll get there. Eventually."

"When this is over, when we've got Sybil home again, safe and sound, how about you and I take a few days to ourselves?"

"Serious?"

"We can leave Kenny and Bea in charge for forty-eight hours. What would you like to do?"

Nadine pretended to consider the options, but when she finally spoke, he could tell she'd known from the start what she wanted.

"How about we go visit my folks in Helena?"

"Uh…yeah." He shoved a hand through his hair. "Sure. Sounds like fun." Like going to the dentist. Something he had to do but dreaded it all the same.

His relationship with his family was complicated, and in some respects, damaged beyond repair. From Nadine's stories, her folks were different.

But meeting them…a whole different story. He wanted

to turn and run the other way.

✕

JUSTIN ROLLED OVER in bed and took a discreet look at his phone. Nine minutes after one. They'd been in bed for over an hour. Time to stop pretending either one of them could sleep.

"What are you thinking about?"

"Right now?"

Her speedy answer confirmed his suspicion that she'd been awake the entire time.

"Your dad."

Debbie-Ann turned to face him. Thanks to his blackout blinds, he could barely make out her shape. But she felt warm and soft as he pulled her head to his chest. He inhaled the botanical scent of his own shampoo on her silky hair.

"I take it you heard his suggestion that Geneva and I move in with him?"

"I did. How do you feel about the idea?"

"Obviously, not thrilled. Now if the invitation had come from you…"

She gasped softly. "You're not serious."

"I am. Only I think it makes more sense for you and Ash to move here since I've got more room."

"It sounds like you've given this some thought."

"This and a lot of other things." He kissed the top of her

head. “Like getting engaged and doing the whole wedding thing. But don’t take this as my official proposal. I have something much more romantic in mind.”

She placed her hand on his cheek and kissed him. “I’m not going to pretend to be anything but excited about the idea of marrying you and moving in together. But your dad is getting older. And…I don’t want to worry you, but I’m concerned about his health. He’s been losing weight. And his mind doesn’t seem as sharp as it was, either.”

How like Debbie-Ann to put his father’s interests ahead of her own. “Last month he went for his annual medical and was given a clean bill of health. But I agree—something’s wrong. Maybe it’s more mental than physical. He’s lost interest in his old hobbies and friends and seems to be leaning more and more on me.”

“How old is your dad?”

“Not even seventy.”

“That’s still relatively young. Maybe he shouldn’t have retired. Now that you’re healthy and don’t need as much of his help, he no longer has a purpose.”

She was giving him the perfect segue. And maybe now was a good time. He didn’t feel at all tired. “About the clinic closing…there’s some family stuff I want to share with you. Should we get into it now, or would you rather sleep?”

“Now,” she answered promptly. “I’m not a bit tired.”

To prove it, she reached over and turned on the bedside lamp, twisting the knob until it reached the dimmest setting.

They both scooched up to sitting positions, resting their backs against the padded headboard.

Justin took one of her hands, suddenly unsure how to start.

"Does this have something to do with finding out Rosemary was your biological mother?"

"Very perceptive."

"Not really. It was a major bombshell. I would have asked more questions if so much else wasn't happening at the same time."

This was true. Marsha's suicide. Her attempted murder of Rosemary and Tiff. Those had all, rightfully so, taken center stage.

Justin squeezed her hand a little tighter. "Let me go back to the day I was born. It was winter and there was a big blizzard. The mountain pass was closed, so Lost Trail was effectively cut off from the rest of the world."

"What a scary time to go into labor."

"It was. And it happened to two women on the same night. My supposed mother, Franny Pittman, and my biological mother, Rosemary Masterson. They were both in the clinic, where my father was the doctor and Marsha Holmes—Rosemary's sister—was the nurse."

"Was Rosemary's husband there too?"

"No. Irving Masterson was caught on the wrong side of the pass when the storm hit. I suppose Rosemary was glad she had her sister, at least. But it turned out to be a terrible thing. Because after the babies were born, and my father saw that the smaller boy had a heart defect, Marsha managed to switch the babies, so Franny had the healthy boy and Rosemary the one with the defective heart."

"How…evil." Debbie-Ann shifted closer to him. "Whenever I took Ashley to the clinic, I always hoped we'd get the other nurse, Farrah Saddler. Something about Marsha rubbed me the wrong way. But how could she do such a thing to her own sister?"

"She was bitterly jealous of Rosemary. I guess she'd been in love with Irving too. But he chose Rosemary. Marsha also resented the fact that their parents had given Raven Farm to Rosemary and Irving to run rather than her."

"Didn't her parents leave Marsha anything?"

"A sizeable nest egg, so I've heard. But that wasn't enough for Marsha. She had a toxic resentment about what she saw as her sister's golden life, so when she had a chance to hurt her, she took it."

"So far this is pretty much the story that went circulating around town after Marsha died. But I always wondered how Marsha was able to switch the babies without your father figuring it out."

"That's the thing I want you to know. The official story is that my father didn't realize what Marsha did. But of course, he did. He'd delivered the babies. How could he not see that the boy his wife was holding was not the same child he'd delivered a few hours ago?"

“Oh man.” Her voice was shaky. “Of course, you’re right. He had to have known.” She let her head drop onto his shoulder. “You must have been so angry when you found out.”

“I was. I still am. Because of him I never got to be with my real biological family.” Fury churned inside of him, eating at him, a cancer of a different sort than the one that had been eradicated. He took a deep breath. Forced his voice lower. “And yet, this man raised me. In every other way was a good father. I let him help me when I was going through my cancer treatment. Now that he’s the one who needs me, is it fair for me to turn my back?”

Chapter Ten

May 4

WEST OFF THE 93 onto Montana State road 43 was the way to Wisdom, but Nadine and Zak weren't going that far today. Out the passenger window of Zak's new vehicle—a.k.a. the sheriff-mobile—Nadine surveyed a landscape much like the one she'd enjoyed so much on Thursday: rocky, semi-arid land dressed up for spring with leafy shrubs, bright yellow arrowleaf balsamroot, and the ubiquitous, rusty-barked ponderosa pine.

They were en route to visit Dr. Zane Elser, Zak obviously pumped about the prospect of finding Sybil and returning her to safety.

Nadine figured their odds for success were about fifty-fifty.

She sighed, shifted her position so her legs were crossed away from Zak.

"What's the matter?" Zak had both hands on the wheel, and he spared her only a short glance. "You hardly ate any breakfast, now it seems like you can't sit still. Leather seats not comfortable enough? Try adjusting your lumbar support."

Making fun of the extra features Archie Ford had purchased with taxpayer money for his official vehicle was something both she and Zak enjoyed doing. She bet Ford never guessed when he made the expenditure two years ago that it would be Zak, not him, putting the majority of the miles on the upscale Tahoe.

"Lumbar support is fine, thanks. I'm just restless, I guess." She hadn't slept well, professional and private concerns tangled like barbed wire in her racing mind.

Zak slowed as the posted sign for Bitterroot Big Hole Road came into view. He turned the sheriff-mobile left, onto a graveled road that curved like a river through the wilderness. Out here there were no signs of human occupation. Last time they'd seen a house was when they'd turned off the 93.

Nadine was staring out the side window again when Zak abruptly hit the brakes. She grabbed the dash.

"Sorry," he said.

Ahead on the road was a black mama bear trailed by two cubs. The sow lifted her nose as she took a good whiff of the Tahoe. The babies tottering behind her looked as fluffy and soft as kittens.

"Wow, how cute!" Though black bears and grizzlies thrived in these parts, Nadine didn't often get a chance to view them up close. Being safely ensconced in the truck meant she could relax and reach for her phone to snap some pictures.

Finally the mama bear moved on, crossing into the forest on the other side of the road, her babies close behind.

"That reminds me." Zak pressed on the gas as he brought the Tahoe back to speed. "We need to get someone out to Loon Lake soon."

This time of year bears were a problem in the cottage community at the north side of the lake, where luxury cabins sat next to bare-bones wooden cabins. All it took were a few families leaving their garbage in unsecure containers to habituate the hungry bears to human food.

"I meant to do that on Thursday. Before I got the call about Sybil." Which reminded her of Amber. The young girl had been on her mind a lot last night when she wasn't sleeping. "Do you know anything about the Woodrow family?"

"Peter Woodrow? With the farm off South Boundary Road? Yeah, I know him."

She shook her head in amazement. "Do you know everyone in this county?"

"Pretty much. Most everyone shopped in my dad's hardware store at one time or another."

Nadine checked out Zak's profile. Sure enough, his jaw was clenched, and his shoulders were tight. Usually any mention of his family—especially his father—got him tense. Then again, they were about ten minutes from Zane Elser's home. So, it could be that, too.

"I met his daughter the other day when I was on patrol. I stopped and asked for some water. She offered me lemonade. I think she must be lonely, living way out there. The closest neighbor is five miles away."

"I remember when Peter's wife died. It was pretty ugly. Her hair got caught in the auger at harvest time."

Nadine stared at him, horrified by the picture those few words planted in her brain. Poor, poor Amber. "Who was with her?"

"Her husband and her son, Ian. Sheriff Ford went out to investigate and I wrote up his report. Seems the father blamed himself for the accident. He said something funny, distracted his wife at just the wrong time."

So they'd been the kind of family who liked to have fun when they worked. That made the accident seem all the more tragic. "No wonder Peter Woodrow started drinking."

"Is that what he's doing?"

"According to his daughter." Nadine was about to mention the bruises on Amber's wrists, when a double-wide mobile home came into view, about a hundred yards off the main road. The home was set in a small clearing in the forest, with no maintained lawn or garden. A dark gray truck was parked a short distance from the main door. Looked like it needed a wash.

Zak parked at the top of the lane, behind a grove of cottonwoods, growing alongside the bank of a creek. He killed the engine. "You notice any dogs?"

"Not yet." Nadine pulled a couple of dried elk liver strips from her pocket. "But I'm prepared."

"You win. My Milk Bone biscuits pale in comparison."

Nadine undid her seat belt and heard Zak do the same. She turned to him.

"You ready?" He held her gaze steady, until she gave the nod. Then they checked their guns and left the vehicle, closing the doors quietly.

Nadine followed Zak toward the house. No dogs ran out to meet them. All Nadine could hear was the busy chatter of chickadees and nuthatches. A squirrel ran the length of a long tree branch, then sat up and scolded them. From somewhere in the highest of treetops a bird called out something that sounded like *hebejebe*.

"That's a ruby-crowned kinglet," Zak said quietly.

"Does it bite?"

He smiled, and her heart did a happy flip. She liked making Zak smile.

The house was about twenty feet away now. Thanks to the bright morning sun, they couldn't see inside the windows, couldn't even tell if the curtains were drawn or not.

No outbuildings were on the property, not even a garage. The truck seemed to match Ellie Somers's vague description. Nadine made note of the plates, as Zak checked the tread on the tires.

"Not the same vehicle. This one still has winter tires. With studs."

Zak's tone was matter-of-fact but Nadine could tell he was disappointed.

They approached the front door together and Zak gave a firm series of three knocks.

The front door opened so quickly, Zane must have been standing on the other side, waiting.

He was a medium-height, portly man. His beard and hair were mostly gray and in need of a trim. He wore a University of Montana sweatshirt and gray sweatpants with elasticized ankles. His feet were bare, revealing pale toes with overgrown nails.

In contrast, the tabby cat he was holding was perfectly groomed.

Zak made introductions and showed his badge. "And you are Zane Elser?"

"*Dr.* Elser." The man had eyes like brown marbles…round and inclined to roll around a lot.

"We're investigating the disappearance of a woman we believe you met on the Montana Matches Website." Zak paused for a long moment. Nadine sensed he was hoping Elser would feel compelled to fill the silence, and maybe say more than he intended.

But Elser seemed perfectly content to wait out the sheriff.

Finally, Zak pulled out a photograph of Sybil. "I believe you know this woman?"

Elser took a few seconds to examine the picture. "Yeah.

She's the librarian from Lost Trail. Sybil something-or-other." As he spoke, a second cat came into the room, this one black and sleek. The cat brushed by Nadine's leg—once and then again. Nadine crouched so she could scratch behind her pert little ears.

Some of the tension left Elser's face. "Like cats, do you?"

"Actually, I'm more of a horse and dog woman. The sheriff here is the one who loves cats."

Elser turned from her to Zak. "If this is going to take more than a few minutes, maybe we should sit down."

There was no need to ask where to sit. A sofa and two chairs were positioned in a semicircle to the left of the entrance. Across from the seating arrangement was a large-screen TV and next to that, an overstuffed bookshelf. A second glance at the bookshelf revealed a third cat. This one with long gray hair and a very sweet little face.

Three cats. No wonder Elser didn't have a dog.

Nadine and Zak took the chairs, leaving the sofa for Elser. As she sank into the large leather chair, Nadine scanned the room searching for signs of Sybil's possible presence. There was a single glass on the coffee table. The brown leather slippers next to the sofa were too large to be worn by a woman. Nothing unusual.

She glanced into the adjoining room. In what would usually be a dining area was a large wooden desk and a matching credenza. Besides a laptop computer, there were orderly stacks of books and papers on the desk.

Elser followed her gaze. "I'm working on a book. It's my retirement project."

That could explain why he'd chosen to live way out here.

"Maybe we can settle this quickly and be on our way," Zak said. "Where were you around six thirty on Thursday evening?"

Zane stroked the tabby curled up next to him on the sofa. He took a few moments to reply, but when he finally spoke, he was once again the snooty academic. "I was where I am most evenings. Here, at home, preparing my dinner. I always dine at seven o'clock."

"And before that?" Zak pressed.

"Working on my book. I save my document on Dropbox every fifteen minutes. You can check the time stamps on my computer."

"Sure. I'd like to see that if you don't mind." Zak's friendly tone made it seem he was interested in how the process worked.

As Elser went to sit at his desk, Nadine and Zak followed, stooping so they could see the screen.

Elser tapped a key and the computer came to life, revealing, not the book he was supposedly working on, but a chat site. He quickly closed that down then opened his Dropbox and scrolled to the history of a document titled, *World Anarchy: It Could Happen.*

On the date that Sybil disappeared the save dates on the computer suggested Elser had worked from one in the afternoon until six p.m.

"See?" Elser sounded triumphant.

Nadine turned to Zak and raised her eyebrows skeptically. This was a laptop. For all they knew he could have taken it with him when he went to Sybil's house.

He seemed to be thinking along the same lines. "Do you ever work outside your home? I've heard some writers like to work in libraries or coffee shops."

"Sometimes. But not that day." Elser's small eyes rolled between the two of them, reflecting a sudden uncertainty.

"Okay, so just to clarify things for me," Zak said. "When is the last time you spoke to Sybil Tombe?"

"That would be over a month ago. We met in Hamilton for a coffee. To tell you the truth, she wasn't my type. We never had a second date."

"You say she wasn't your type. Does that mean you never asked for a second date?"

"Well, maybe I suggested it. Just to be polite."

"Suggested once?"

"Okay. A few times." Elser's face reddened. "When she turned me down I was actually relieved. There are plenty of other women interested in connecting with successful, educated men."

Nadine fought the impulse to roll her eyes. "Anyway, she was probably too old for you. Don't you prefer your women much younger? Like Caitlin Carter?"

Elser's eyebrows shot together. "What the hell? Is that

why you guys are out here? Damn it, that accusation was totally spurious. And yet the cloud keeps hanging over my head. I guess innocent until proven guilty no longer applies in America."

Nadine leaned forward. "Innocent? Is that how you feel when you chat with young women while you're pretending to be a thirty-five-year-old man?"

That took the hot air out of his balloon. As Elser sank back into his chair, Nadine was tempted to press him about his evening activities. But lying about your age and chatting up young women on the internet wasn't a crime.

When it was time to leave, Nadine asked if she could use the facilities. Elser wasn't pleased, but he pointed out the door. As she headed toward the hall Nadine heard Zak engage Elser with questions about his book. Taking advantage of the distraction, Nadine glanced into the kitchen.

A bowl and a mug—remnants from breakfast—were stacked next to the sink. Otherwise the room was quite tidy. There were three closed doors off the hall, presumably two bedrooms, in addition to the bathroom. If he turned his head, Elser would see her, so she didn't dare check the bedrooms. But she did listen carefully before entering the bathroom.

Grime had collected around the faucet and the bathtub had a dark ring around the high-water mark, but other than that the room was reasonably clean. Not being a clean freak herself, Nadine thought for a single man living on his own,

Elser was reasonably hygienic.

She flushed the toilet. Ran the water for twenty seconds. Then turned out the light and left the room. When Zak glanced at her, she raised her eyebrows. *All clear.*

If Elser had anything to do with Sybil's disappearance, there was nothing here to show it.

Chapter Eleven

IN CONJUNCTION WITH her mom, Tiff came up with the plan to invite Justin and Geneva to Raven Farm for lunch. After they ate, Rosemary would suggest making cookies and Geneva would jump all over the idea. She loved baking with her grandmother. At that point, Tiff would take Justin outside for a walk and discuss the tricky situation with Clark.

Tiff was anxious about how Justin would react. He was kindhearted and loyal—a lot like their mother. But there was a limit to how much a person could forgive. She hoped he would understand that.

Sybil's disappearance was the main topic over lunch. Everyone was careful not to alarm Geneva by expressing their true fears, but the worry was evident, especially on Tiff's mother's face. Every few minutes Rosemary would check her phone, obviously hoping for news.

But there was none.

Finally the meal was over.

"Does anyone want to bake cookies?" Rosemary asked.

"I do!" Geneva bounced out of her chair.

"I don't," said her father.

"Daddy only bakes pancakes and waffles," Geneva explained. Then she patted her father's hand. "Maybe you can play with Aunt Tiff while Grandma and I bake?"

Justin winked at Tiff. "How about it, Sis? Want to play?"

Tiff felt a pang of sadness. If not for Clark and Martha's evil scheme, she and Justin would have grown up playing together. Skiing with their parents in the winter, playing kick-the-can and hide-and-seek on the farm. Unlike Casey, Justin wouldn't have had to limit his activities due to his weak heart. He would have kicked her butt at everything.

"It's a beautiful day. Let's go for a walk."

They slipped on their shoes and went out through the patio doors off the kitchen. Tiff whistled for Spade to join them. The old dog came trotting—he'd been a lot happier since Tiff had moved back home.

Now that she was here, Tiff wondered how she had stayed away for so long. Working on the farm, being close to her mother again, her relationship with Kenny—all these had given her a level of happiness she hadn't experienced since Casey's death.

"I take it you have something you want to talk about?"

Justin was dressed in jeans, white trainers and a blue polo shirt. His build—tall, slim-hipped, broad-shouldered—was so like her father's it was a wonder no one had spotted the deception sooner. And, like her father, her brother was a handsome man. Even more so since his curly blond hair had grown back.

"I do. We can talk in Dad's old office in the barn. Or go for a walk. Which do you prefer?"

"I'd like to see the office."

"Okay."

Justin asked questions about the Christmas tree farming business, and so Tiff told him about the new variety they were planting this year, their struggles with the bark beetle and the market gains they'd been experiencing since she'd expanded their website.

In the office Justin was drawn to their father's old walnut desk. He placed his hands flat on the scarred surface. For a few seconds he stood there, head bowed, lost in thought. Then he straightened.

"So how do you like running the farm? Do you miss the accounting firm in Seattle?"

"I love it here," she said simply. If circumstances had been different it could have been Justin, not her, heading the family business. Another "what-if" they would never know the answer to.

"I'm glad for you."

Tiff went to the window and looked out at the fields, a sight she'd grown up with, a sight Justin should have grown up with too. "We can't do anything about the missing years. But Mom and I are your family now. And you have as much right to Raven Farm as I do."

"Aw, Tiff, you've done so much for me already. The

stem-cell transfer…how can I ever repay that? The way you've welcomed Geneva and me into the family. It all means so much. I wouldn't ever want a piece of Raven Farm. I've got my own career, and honestly I'm happy being a lawyer."

"I'm glad, but my offer still stands." She fell silent, all too aware that time was passing, and she still hadn't broached the most difficult subject.

"You want to talk about Clark?"

"Yes." She took a deep breath, grateful to him for getting her started. "Mom's worked hard to forgive him for what he did, or at least what he knew. But lately she's been wondering if he might have been more involved in Marsha's crime than he let on. I have to admit, I've been wondering the same thing for a lot longer."

"Me, too," Justin admitted.

"Really?"

"Dad's been acting strange lately. Not right in the head."

"How so?"

"He's lost interest in his old hobbies and friends. He spends too much time alone, on long drives or walks. He isn't eating properly and he's losing weight. I could go on and on. The latest thing that's happened is he wants me and Geneva to move in with him."

"Seriously? What does Debbie-Ann think about that?"

"She says now that I'm recovered and don't need his help as much, my dad is feeling unwanted. Personally, I wonder if the guilt is getting to him."

Tiff doubted that. She didn't think Clark was capable of guilt. "Maybe he sees how close you and Debbie-Ann are getting and he's afraid of losing you."

"That could be," Justin admitted.

"You don't owe him anything Justin. And frankly, neither do we. Mom's been giving the situation a lot of thought. She's decided Clark is no longer welcome at Raven Farm. I totally support her, and I hope you will too. I also hope you and Geneva will continue coming for Sunday dinners without Clark."

Justin looked uncomfortable. "I understand how you guys feel. But it's harder for me. It's going to crush him if I tell him that."

"The stakes could get a lot bigger than giving up Sunday dinners, Justin. Mom's considering telling the whole story to Zak. You know Clark could go to jail for what he did."

Justin's face paled. "What he did was illegal. And cruel. But I wish you wouldn't go that far. It won't change anything. What's done is done."

Tiff kept her gaze on her brother's face. "Mom and I don't want to hurt you. But we've tried to live with this, tried to forgive, and it just isn't working. We think Clark should pay for what he did."

"Oh, God." Justin dug his hands into his hair and gave his head a shake. "I get how you feel. I do. I'm pretty damn mad at him myself."

He crossed the room to the window and looked out at the rows and rows of conifers, stretching out for miles, representing years of planning and work and hope for the future.

"It's more complicated for you," Tiff acknowledged.

"Yes. In many ways Clark was a good father to me. But he deprived me of my true, biological family. And that, I'm finding, is essentially unforgivable. But prison? I have a hard time with that, too. But it's not my decision, is it?"

"Mom will take your opinion into account. If you tell her to keep quiet—"

"Let me think on it, okay? Maybe I can come up with another solution."

ZAK AND NADINE were back at the office when Kenny phoned in. Zak put the call on speakerphone and waved Nadine into his office. They both sat at the table and listened as Kenny shared his impressions of the third man on their suspect list.

"Jeffery Taylor was polite and cooperative. But he was fidgety, kept losing his focus when he answered questions."

"Could be guilt," Nadine said.

"Or concern about Sybil," Zak was compelled to point out. "Did he account for his time the day Sybil was abducted?"

"Yeah. Interesting thing. There were no classes Thursday and Friday. Teacher organizational days or something. Taylor said he held a staff meeting from eight a.m. until eleven a.m., then worked in his office until three."

Zak's interest perked up. "Can anyone confirm that?"

"Lots of people were at the meeting, so that was easy to verify. But later, Taylor didn't see anyone."

"So conceivably he could have left the office earlier than three." Even if he'd stayed at the office until noon Taylor would have had time to drive to Lost Trail by three o'clock and break into Sybil's house. "What kind of vehicle does Taylor drive?"

Dry laugh from Kenny. "A pickup truck, of course. A Tacoma. Black and clean as a whistle. Looked like it had been washed within the last day or two."

"Did you check the treads?"

"Yeah. All seasons. Taylor agreed to let me take an impression. I'm going to drop it off at the lab with the rest of the evidence."

Zak rubbed his face. They had a description of a man that matched about 50 percent of the older males in this county and a description of a truck that matched about 50 percent of the vehicles those men liked to drive. Didn't narrow the field much.

"So Taylor had the opportunity," Nadine recapped. "And he and his truck meet the general description we have from Sybil's neighbor. What else have we got? If Taylor took her, where is she now? Did you get a good look at his home?"

"He invited me in for coffee, so yeah I got a look. Classic brick house in the university district. He's got lots of art on the walls and expensive-looking carpets on the hardwood floors. I admired the house and get this—he offered me a tour. I guess the house was built by some famous architect and he's super proud of it. Anyway, I checked in all the rooms, even the basement. I'm pretty sure he couldn't be hiding her anywhere on the premises."

Zak had to say it. "Assuming she's alive."

There was a moment of silence. Then Kenny said, solemnly, "Yeah."

This was the ugly possibility they had to consider. If Sybil had been killed, her remains could be anywhere. With so much wilderness all around them, it was possible she might never be found.

"I've already dropped the evidence at the lab," Kenny said. "Should be back in the office in a few hours."

"Great. I've put a list of Sybil's closest friends on your desk. Rosemary Masterson talked to all of them on the phone, but I'd like you to pay each a personal visit and get statements. When did they last see Sybil? Was she upset or worried about anything? Did she mention any new people in her life? That kind of thing."

"Got it."

Once Kenny was off the line, Nadine sank into one of

the chairs at the table. "I'm getting nowhere with the fingerprints, Zak. Kenny tested everything he could think of, from doorknobs to light switches, the fridge, table…everything. And only one set of prints is coming up. Sybil's."

"Our perp wore gloves. Or he wiped down everything he touched. He wasn't a sloppy guy."

"No…but shouldn't there be prints from Sybil's friends? She must have had people to her house occasionally. Why wouldn't they leave prints?"

"That is curious."

"I'm not sure if it's relevant, but I'd like to talk to her neighbor again. And to Rosemary. If Sybil never had people to her house…maybe there's a reason?"

"Yes. Good idea. Meanwhile I'm going to drive to Bozeman."

Nadine did a double take. "I thought you were getting the authorities over there to question Martin Thomson?"

"They did. I just had a report from a Sergeant Carson. Martin drives a dark blue Dodge Ram, so his vehicle fits. In his favor though, he's clean-shaven, plus he claims he had a client meeting that took the entire day."

Nadine's shoulders slumped. "So that clears him."

"Yeah. If he didn't have a beard he recently shaved off. And if his alibi is solid and he didn't just ask a friend to cover for him. I won't be sure of those answers unless I go down to Bozeman and speak to Martin and his business clients personally."

"You couldn't ask Carson to do that?"

"If this case wasn't so important, I would."

Nadine unfolded her long body from the chair and stood with a weary sigh. "You're right. You need to go. Kenny and I will hold down things here."

Chapter Twelve

IT WAS ALMOST a four-hour drive to Bozeman, eight hours round trip, and it might all prove a colossal waste of time, but Sybil had been missing two days now and time was their enemy.

Every day in America adults voluntarily disappeared, for various, personal reasons. But not in this case. The evidence might be circumstantial—the anonymous letter, the missing spare key, Sybil's wallet and cell phone on the foyer floor—but it was supported by everything Zak knew about Sybil, her character, her habits and routines, her personality.

He had no doubt that her disappearance had been involuntary.

What he didn't know was why she had been taken, or by whom. Was her life in jeopardy? Was she already dead?

He had so little to go on, all he could do was follow each lead, no matter how slim.

He stopped at home to put out food for Watson and throw together an overnight bag. Then he made a quick pit stop at the Snowdrift for coffee and a sandwich…and hell, yes, he was going for the scone, too. Rhubarb and white chocolate today.

A teenaged girl stood behind the counter. Patsy generally took the weekend afternoons off to spend with her family.

"Have you found our librarian yet, Sheriff?" the girl asked as she handed over the paper bag with his food.

He wasn't surprised by the question. He imagined Sybil's disappearance was the number one topic of conversation in the county. "Working on it."

"Well, I hope you find her. My friends and I were in the library on Thursday. Ms. Tombe helped us pick out some really cool books for our English class book reports. She's a really nice lady."

Zak's throat thickened. He bet there wasn't a person in town who had a negative thing to say about Sybil. "We won't rest till we find her."

THERE WERE CERTAIN people in Lost Trail you could not visit without being offered refreshments. Rosemary Masterson was one of these people and Nadine wasn't complaining. She generally preferred dark chocolate, but Rosemary's white chocolate chip and macadamia nut cookies were incredible.

After she finished two, Rosemary offered her more.

"I really shouldn't." She and Zak had grabbed chips and a cola at the gas station after they returned from questioning Zane Elser. When Nadine considered the sweet muffin she'd eaten for breakfast, she literally hadn't eaten any nutritious food all day.

"Thanks Rosemary." The third cookie tasted as good as the first. That was it. No more junk food going forward.

"Any news about Sybil?" Tiff finally asked.

The three of them were sitting at the island in the Mastersons' kitchen. Eau-de-home-baked cookies hung in the air. Nadine's timing had been perfect as two trays had been pulled from the oven since she arrived.

"We're working several angles." Nadine wished she had something concrete to offer. "Right now we're trying to establish who Sybil might have had in her house the last week or two." She pressed her finger over some crumbs on her plate and popped them into her mouth. "I'm hoping you can help us with that."

Rosemary's hair was in a messy bun, a look that accentuated her fine facial structure, but also the lines and gentle sagging of skin around her eyes and jawline.

Tiff hadn't said much, but she watched her mother protectively. Nadine couldn't blame her. Being involved in a crime investigation concerning her best friend was not only scary for Rosemary, it probably also dredged up a lot of painful memories.

"Sybil doesn't entertain at her home. She deals with people all day long at the library, and while she loves her job, she likes her evenings at home to be quiet."

"But sometimes she must have a few friends over? Can

you remember the last time she did that?"

"Hm. Good question." Rosemary's gaze drifted to the left. After a few seconds, her forehead creased, and she frowned. "I'm sorry. I really can't remember."

"Have you *ever* been in Sybil's house?"

"I've dropped things off now and then. Books, extra rhubarb or raspberries from my garden. But now that you mention it, she's never invited me inside for an extended period of time."

"I thought the two of you were good friends?"

"Best of friends. But Sybil always came here. Or we met at the Snowdrift for coffee. Or the library."

"What about your book club? Do you take turns hosting the meetings?"

"We do. But when it was Sybil's turn, we always met at the library. She said it was more comfortable than her small house."

"You must have been to Sybil's house sometimes," Tiff said. "Maybe just for a cup of coffee?"

"You'd think so. But I can't remember a single occasion."

"I talked to her neighbor, Ellie Somers, before I came here," Nadine offered. "She, too, describes Sybil as friendly and sociable—yet she couldn't remember the last time she noticed Sybil entertain any visitors."

"I visit Sybil often," Tiff said. "But always at the library."

"Was she ashamed of her home, do you think? Because it

was so much smaller than yours?"

Both Tiff and Rosemary shook their heads.

"Sybil isn't like that," Tiff said. "She doesn't judge people by how much money they have, or the labels of their clothes, or anything like that. She's very down-to-earth."

"There must be some reason she never has visitors. In a town this size...well, it's unusual."

"I agree with you," Tiff said. "It's strange. And I can't come up with anything to explain it."

"I feel so self-centered. And foolish." Rosemary's eyes clouded over with anguish. "I thought she was my best friend. But now it seems like I barely knew her."

IT WAS ALMOST eight at night when Zak arrived in Bozeman. Not too late to call on the client who'd provided Martin Thomson with his alibi for Thursday afternoon and evening.

Zak punched the address he'd been given into the nav system. Rick Wright lived in a new subdivision just off Interstate 90. It was a large house, with western architectural touches like a metal roof and river rock chimney.

Of more relevance were the two pickup trucks parked out front of the double garage: one dark blue, one gray.

The plates on the dark blue one matched those provided by Carson. What luck, he was getting two interviews for the price of one.

Before heading to the front door, Zak checked the tread on the tires of both trucks. Martin Thomson still had his winter tires on. The other truck had all seasons, looked like they could match. Lucky Rick Wright just became a person of interest.

A woman appearing to be in her late forties answered the door, holding a remote control. She was dressed for comfort in a baggy sweatshirt and skintight leggings. Messy hair, no makeup, but judging by her polished, long nails, she generally took some pains with her appearance.

Zak could hear the TV going and the smell of microwaved popcorn hung in the air.

"Good evening, I'm Sheriff Zak Waller of Lost Trail County."

"You're not old enough to be a sheriff."

Zak showed her his badge. Noticing her wedding band and flashy diamond he asked, "Are you Rick Wright's wife?"

"I'm the lucky one," she agreed in a tone that implied the opposite. "First name Sherry. Want me to call him up for you? He and his buddy Marty are in the basement playing video games and getting drunk. The usual."

She didn't seem too concerned that a sheriff stood on her front doorstep. Either she had a clean conscience, or she didn't care, period. For the moment it seemed like a good idea to keep her talking. "Good friends, are they?"

"They've known each other since high school." Sherry rolled her eyes. "Always act like teenagers when Marty rolls into town. Which he does far too often, if you ask me."

"Do you remember what day Martin came to town this time?"

"It was Thursday."

"You're sure?"

She nodded. "When Rick called me to say they were going out, I was at the salon. I work at the Diva Salon and Spa on Tuesdays and Thursdays."

"What time did he call, do you remember?"

"Not sure. It was before lunch."

"And when did they make it home?"

"They didn't. Rick's got a fishing cabin on the West Gallatin River. He and Marty went out there for the night. They planned on staying the entire weekend, but I guess they didn't pack enough beer or something."

Or something.

"Could I talk to Rick for a minute?"

"Sure. I'll call him up."

"That's okay. I'll go down."

He really wanted to see what was in the basement.

RICK WRIGHT'S BASEMENT was the ultimate in man caves, filled with 'boy toys' including two large-screen TVs, one meant for watching, the other for video games, plus a pool table and a stack of pornographic magazines by the sofa.

Judging by the look and the smell of the dimly lit, carpeted room, it wasn't cleaned all that often.

Two men were seated at the sofa in front of the second TV, game consoles in hand and about a dozen open beer cans on the coffee table in front of them. The shorter, clean-shaven man put down his game console when he noticed Zak.

"What the hell? Is this about that missing librarian again? She wasn't even my type."

Zak produced his badge and gave his name again. Funny how quickly some men wanted to call a woman 'not my type' after the woman turned them down. But he'd read the messages and so he knew it was Martin Thomson who hadn't been Sybil's type. He could see why Sybil had agreed to the first date, though. Martin was a good-looking man, his features reminiscent of the Scottish actor who'd once played James Bond.

"Yes, I'm looking into the disappearance of Sybil Tombe." He glanced at Wright. Sherry's husband was a good ten years older than her, taller than Martin, with a full beard that was two shades grayer than his hair.

"Well I haven't seen that…lady…in over a month. I explained this already."

"I've driven a long way to talk to you in person. So, I'd like to hear it again. What were you doing two days ago, on Thursday?"

Martin swore. "Like I told the other guy, me and Rick

had a business meeting. Then we stocked up on some supplies and drove out to his cabin to do some fishing."

That wasn't quite what Carson had reported. Why was Martin changing his story now? In the far corner Zak spied a gun cabinet and several shelves of fishing gear.

As he looked the guns over, Zak asked in a casual tone, "I notice your trucks are parked outside. You won't mind if I take impressions of the tires?"

The men grumbled, but finally followed him outside, waiting as he inked the front driver's side tire, which was the one Kenny had got the casting from. Then he had them drive over special paper made for the purpose. As he waited for the impressions to dry, he carried on with his questions.

"Did you see anyone when you were at the cabin? Someone who could corroborate your whereabouts?"

The two men exchanged glances. Zak's bullshit monitor went up.

"Nope. Didn't see anyone," Martin finally said. "We fished all day, drank all night, then got up in the morning, ate cold pizza for breakfast, and drove home."

"Mind if I take a look at this cabin?"

"What the hell you want to do that for?" Rick's tone was defensive, bordering on angry. "We don't got any librarians stashed out there, if that's what you're thinking."

Could they have done this together? They were definitely acting guilty about something. "In that case, you shouldn't mind me having a look."

Zak glanced at the sky. Soon it would be getting dark. "Tomorrow morning at seven thirty work for you guys?"

Neither one answered, but Rick gave a short nod.

May 5

EARLY THE NEXT morning, after a marginal night's sleep at a discount hotel, Zak drove back to Wright's home, first stopping for a sausage and egg biscuit and a large coffee. As he paid for his breakfast he thought of the green smoothies and omelets that had been his norm in the pre-sheriff days.

No wonder his pants were getting tight.

Marty and Rick took some prodding to get going, but they were all on the road before eight, Zak following about ten car lengths behind Rick's pickup.

The cabin made Rick's basement look like a finished Marie Kondo project. Everywhere was evidence of binge drinking, and the aroma of pot still clung to the air.

Was a little weed the reason the guys seemed so uptight?

Zak inspected the three-room cabin with an eye to finding a link to Sybil. In the main living area he opened the potbelly stove. Just ashes. Stacked among the wood and kindling next to the stove were some rolled-up newspaper sheets.

Thursday's paper, he noted.

Behind him, hanging out by the door, looking like they

were considering making a run for it, were the two older men. Still looking guilty as hell.

It was a curious thing, how a uniform and a badge could make bigger and older men cower. Too bad he hadn't had these things when he was a kid dealing with his old man and brothers.

Zak moved to the bedroom. Two queen beds pretty much filled the space. The bedding was rumpled and had a nasty, musty odor. Zak checked the closet. Under the door. Nothing but dust and a single wool sock. He was about to leave when he decided to pull back the comforters. In one of the beds was a pair of women's panties, mostly string with a little triangle of red fabric.

Zak unholstered his gun and used it to snag the panties. Then he carried the prize out to the main room. "These don't look like they'd fit either of you."

The guys were not amused.

"Must be the wife's." Rick made a show of straightening the waders piled next to the door.

"Comes out here often, does she? No wonder the place is decorated so nice." Zak's gaze went from a pile of porno magazines, to a case of empty beer cans, to a pile of bedding on the sofa.

"Don't go dragging Sherry into this." Marty combed his slick hair with his fingers. "Maybe we had some women join us out here. That isn't a crime."

Zak stared from one man to the next. They'd had a party, drank some beer, done some drugs, and maybe even paid for a prostitute or two. That's what the evidence told him. None of this ruled out the possibility that they'd taken a detour to Lost Trail Thursday afternoon. Rick had a beard and the right sort of tires. He could be the man who ambushed Sybil.

It was all possible. But unlikely.

Zak flicked the undies to the floor and reholstered his gun. Sybil wasn't here. Which meant he had to stop wasting his time with these charming gentlemen and get on his way.

Chapter Thirteen

ZAK SPENT MOST of the drive back to Lost Trail on the phone. First with Kenny who reported on his progress getting statements from Sybil's friends.

"I went out to the Lazy S to talk to Vanessa Stillman."

The cellular connection was faint, but audible. "You sure you mean Vanessa, not Em?"

The Lazy S was the largest ranch in Lost Trail County. Since Lacy Stillman's death, the ranch had been managed primarily by her sons Clayton and Eugene. Clayton's wife Vanessa, who loved shopping and spa days more than cattle or horseback riding, wasn't someone Zak would have guessed to be in Sybil's inner circle. Eugene's hardworking, down-to-earth wife Em, however, was another matter.

"I spoke to both Em and Vanessa," Kenny clarified, his voice coming in clearer as Zak crested a major hill.

Zak took a bite of the burger he'd bought for lunch. "Go on."

"Em didn't have much to say, other than she was shocked and worried. Vanessa said virtually the same things but with a lot more drama."

Didn't sound too helpful so far. "And?"

"Vanessa's daughter Nikki was in the kitchen while we were talking. She seemed pretty interested in the conversation but didn't say anything. Later, as I was leaving, she ran up to me just before I got in my truck."

Zak knew Nikki fairly well as she was only a few years younger than him, plus he was good friends with her cousin Luke. Unlike her mother, Nikki was devoted to the ranch and her family's legacy meant everything to her. This caused frequent family clashes. He wasn't surprised Nikki hadn't spoken to Kenny in front of her mother.

"What did Nikki have to say?"

"She was in the library on Thursday afternoon. She thought Sybil seemed sad and she asked how she was feeling. Sybil seemed surprised that she asked. Nikki had the impression she was going to put on a fake smile and say she was fine, but then Sybil leaned forward and said in a very quiet voice that the beginning of May was a hard time for her."

Interesting. Most people looked forward to May and the end of the long winter. "Did she say why?"

"No. Nikki said Sybil changed the subject right away. Seemed almost embarrassed to have said anything at all."

That made sense. Zak was beginning to appreciate that their wonderful librarian had been a lot more private than any of them had guessed. He wasn't surprised that it would be Nikki of all people who would get past her guard. Nikki had a way with people, and she was very intuitive. She'd certainly figured out her grandmother better than anyone else in the family.

Kenny went through the other names on the list. Zak listened carefully but didn't pick up anything that felt relevant to their investigation. Obviously, Kenny felt the same way.

"I've still got six more people to talk to. Should be done by the time you're back in town."

"Thanks, Kenny. I appreciate you working all weekend on this."

"Hey. When you lose someone on the mountain, you don't come down until you find them."

That attitude said a lot about his new deputy. Tiff had picked herself a good man this time. Not that he'd known the last one very well. But living in Seattle was a solid strike against him.

Zak used the Bluetooth to call Nadine next. "Hey, you. How's it going?"

"The critters on the ranch have serious spring fever. I took Making Magic out for an hour this morning, with Junior tagging along. All three of us would have been happy to stay out all day."

"But?"

"I kept thinking of Sybil. I decided to take another look in her house. I focused on her office this time and noticed something odd in her Day-Timer."

He remembered the book she was referring to. Turquoise

blue leather, about eight inches by eleven. "It was on her desk, right? Next to her computer?"

"Yup. It's the kind that has an entire month on every double page. Apparently Sybil used it to keep track of birthdays and anniversaries. Puts the name and the year of birth in the square for the correct date. But one date was different…she filled it with little hearts and colored them in with black ink."

A day filled with black hearts. "Let me guess. Was this in early May?"

"Yes. May fifth. How did you know?"

ZAK WAS ALMOST home when a familiar sedan flew by traveling in the opposite direction. Zak pulled a quick U-turn and peeled off after the guy. He hadn't seen the driver's face clearly—high speed had made that impossible—but he was pretty sure who he was.

His office had issued two speeding tickets to Clark Pittman this winter. Prior to that, his driving record had been clean.

In March Nadine had followed Pittman for ten miles before pulling him over. She said he'd been making erratic speed changes, veering out of his lane…like he was drunk. But when she gave him a breathalyzer, he'd been stone sober.

Zak gained on the sedan until he could read the plate.

Yup this was Pittman. He followed him for almost half a mile before Pittman finally pulled over.

Zak took his time getting out of his truck.

A few years ago he'd looked up to this man. Almost everyone in the community had. He'd been Lost Trail's only doctor, the coroner for the sheriff's department, someone whose opinion mattered and was trusted.

The unraveling had begun years ago with the exposure of Marsha Holmes's secret, but it was quickly getting worse.

He made his way to the driver's side window. The window was already down. Seeing Clark, Zak jerked back. He barely recognized the man. Clark had aged dramatically in the past few months. He'd become smaller, thinner, more wrinkled. Hair once a distinguished gray was now a dirty white, several shades lighter than his scraggly, unkempt beard.

Glad his sunglasses covered his surprise, Zak said, "Did you realize you were driving seventy miles an hour in a fifty zone?"

Pittman didn't look impressed. "What are you doing wasting your time with me? Shouldn't you be out looking for Sybil and the bastard who kidnapped her?"

"Where are you off to in such a hurry?"

"Just out for a drive."

Zak glanced inside the sedan. In the back was a travel blanket and the doctor's old medical kit. A large takeout bag from the Snowdrift Café was on the front passenger seat, along with a pile of papers. The top one had a picture of a country home, followed by a string of data. A real estate listing, Zak realized.

Why was Pittman looking at real estate? He already owned one of the nicest houses in town.

"Registration, insurance, and license."

Clark's lips compressed as he handed over the papers. "On a power trip are you, Zak? I can't believe I once thought you'd make a good sheriff."

Zak fought the urge to reply with a zinger of his own and went back to his vehicle to write out the ticket.

A few minutes later, he handed the papers back to Pittman, along with the ticket. "Watch your speed from now on. Lots of wildlife on the road this time of year."

For a moment their eyes connected. Zak looked deep into the man's dark pupils. *I know what kind of man you are. Don't think I've forgotten.*

FROM HIS FRONT window Justin saw his father drive up to the house. He pulled the lasagna from the oven, then went to open the door. "I was starting to worry."

He was more than an hour late for dinner. And Clark Pittman was never late.

"Sorry, Son. I was out for a drive and time got away from me." His father looked past Justin into the living area.

"Geneva in her room?"

"She's having dinner at Raven Farm tonight." Tiff had come to pick her up a few hours ago. Geneva was thrilled. While he was sick and in the hospital, she'd become very attached to her aunt and grandmother.

"I thought you said Sunday night dinner was canceled?"

Just for you, Dad. "I thought it would be better if Geneva wasn't here tonight. Give us a chance to talk."

His father's face brightened. "About my idea?"

"Among other things. Come on and sit down. We'll let the lasagna set for a few minutes. Can I get you a beer or glass of wine?"

"I'll just have juice if you have it."

"Tomato or apple?"

"Tomato. Maybe with a bit of Tabasco and Worcestershire?"

Justin went to the kitchen and made two virgin Bloody Marys. Then, thinking of all the things he needed to make clear to his father tonight, he added a couple ounces of vodka to his.

"Saw our esteemed sheriff this afternoon." Clark nudged Dora out of the dog's favorite chair and took her place. "I don't think he has a clue what happened to Sybil. I sure was wrong about that boy."

"He's a man, Dad. And more than capable. According to Tiff the entire sheriff's office has been working flat out since Friday. It's such a strange situation. Sybil disappearing into thin air. Someone must have taken her, but who? Everyone in town loves her."

"It'll probably come down to nothing. Sybil went on a trip and forgot to tell anyone."

Justin couldn't understand his lack of concern. "Without her car? Leaving her purse in the house?"

"How do you know that?"

"According to Debbie-Ann, Sybil's neighbor could see Sybil's purse on the floor when she looked in the window, before the sheriff arrived."

"Ellie Somers? That women needed cataract surgery five years ago."

Justin gave his father a closer look. It wasn't like him to be this callous. Or it hadn't been in the past. "I just hope they find her. And soon." He was going to mention the man who'd been seen lurking around the grade school but decided against it. They had enough tough topics to discuss tonight.

Before broaching any of them, though, he wanted to make sure his father ate. He served lasagna and Caesar salad and was gratified when Clark ate healthy portions of each.

"Nice to see you have a good appetite. I've been worried about you."

"Why? I told you about my last checkup. According to my GP I'm in excellent health."

"Then why have you been losing weight?"

"Sometimes I forget to eat. That happens when you live

alone."

"About that—"

"It's not for my sake that I think we should live together." His father leaned forward, his expression animated, almost excited. "I want to be helpful. Just think of the advantages from your point of view. Live-in babysitter for times when you need to work late, or if Geneva has a cold and can't go to school. We could get a bigger home, maybe an acreage with room for some horses. Geneva loves animals."

"Dad, Geneva and I are not leaving this house. If you get to the point where you can't live alone, I'm going to be here for you. But right now, I have different plans for my life."

His father sank back into his chair. "What plans?"

"Debbie-Ann and I plan to get married. Soon," he added, though he hadn't yet given her the ring, let alone set a date.

His father looked flabbergasted. "Married? You want to get married again?"

"I do," Justin said quietly, but firmly.

"After Willow, I would have thought you'd be happy to steer clear of the institution."

"I went into that marriage to help an old friend. And because I wanted a family. A child." Something he'd thought he would never have after his cancer treatments left him sterile. "I realize now that marriage was a mistake. But things are different with Debbie-Ann. We love each other."

"She's good with children. And pleasant. But Debbie-Ann is no beauty and frankly she's rather dull to talk to. You're such a handsome and intelligent man. You could do much better than Debbie-Ann."

Justin wasn't surprised to hear his father's criticisms. Clark had never liked any of the women he dated and he'd absolutely abhorred Willow.

"*I* think she's beautiful inside and out and, frankly, very charming. Plus she makes me very happy and Geneva adores her. For the sake of family harmony, I hope you make an effort to get along."

His father closed his eyes. He was quiet for a long while. Then he sighed. "Please do one thing for me. Don't rush into this."

"Debbie-Ann and I have been friends for years and dating for six months. If we don't know one another by now, we never will."

His father met his gaze squarely. "Just remember who was here for you when you and Geneva needed me. You're my family. All I care about in this world."

Justin shifted uneasily in his chair. When he'd turned down good job offers from law firms in Missoula in order to open his own practice near his father in Lost Trail, his former university roommate, Paul Quinlan, had accused Justin of letting his father control his life. If Paul could hear this conversation right now, no doubt he'd give Justin one of his mocking smirks.

"I appreciate all your help when I was sick. But are you really asking me to give up living with the woman I love in order to pay you back?"

"Is she the woman you love? Are you sure?"

He shook his head. "I can't talk about this with you anymore."

"Fine. Let's leave it for now." His father stood up from the table. "We can talk again next Sunday, after dinner."

"There isn't going to be another Sunday dinner." He'd intended to broach the subject more tactfully. But he'd used up all the tact he had for the evening. "Rosemary asked me to tell you that you're no longer welcome at Raven Farm. She's tried to forgive what happened in the past. But she can't."

For a second, anger flared in his father's eyes. But then his father lowered his head and allowed his shoulders to slump. "I must accept that, I guess. Will we go back to our usual dinners with just you, me and Geneva?"

"No. Geneva and I are going to continue going to Raven Farm on Sundays. Rosemary is my mother, after all. And Tiff is my sister."

His father's nostrils flared. Then he stared down at the table. "Is this your way of cutting me out of your life?"

Part of Justin wished he could. He was tired of dealing with the complicated emotions he had for this man. A lifetime of bedtime stories, playing catch in the park, Sunday morning waffles…those memories could not be erased so easily though.

"I'm not doing that. I just need to make room for the other people I love."

Clark studied his face a long moment, then gave a short nod. He started for the front door, then paused. "Tell me this. Do you think it's possible for a good man to do a bad thing?"

"I do," Justin agreed.

Unfortunately, he was no longer sure the man who had raised him was a good man.

Chapter Fourteen

DINNER WAS LONG over when Kenny showed up at Raven Farm. Tiff had never seen him looking so depleted. "Poor man." She pulled him close in a tight hug. They stood in the foyer that way for a long time.

"Thank you," Kenny finally said. "I needed that."

"I take it there's been no good news about Sybil?"

His shoulders drooped. "Not really. We've talked to the men she met on that dating site. But they don't seem to be involved. Either they have an alibi, or they drive the wrong truck…" He brushed a hand over his face, as if he could rub away exhaustion. "Sorry I missed dinner."

"No problem. We have leftovers if you're interested."

"Definitely."

Kenny followed her to the kitchen. Tiff turned on the lights then went to the fridge to pull out the plate she'd saved for him.

"It's so quiet. Where's your mom?"

"She's gone to bed. Hopefully she's sleeping. It's hard when we're so worried about Sybil. Having Geneva over this evening was a nice distraction."

"I would have liked to be here. That kid is a hoot. But I had interviews booked right through six, and then I thought I better write up my reports while everything was fresh."

"So, you've spoken to everyone on Mom's list?" Tiff put the plate of roast beef, potatoes and brussels sprouts into the microwave.

"All of them. No one was aware of any trips or problems in Sybil's life. They're all as baffled as your mother is about where she could be."

"We all relied so much on her cheerful, helpful personality. I'm so afraid something terrible has happened to her..."

Kenny put an arm around her shoulders. "Don't. We have to keep hoping."

"You're right. But it isn't easy." This would be the fourth night Sybil was gone from the safety of her own home. It was getting harder to believe in a benign reason for her absence.

Kenny took the plate out of the microwave and went to the island to eat. He cut into the beef first. "This smells great."

Tiff perched on the stool next to him. "I just got off the phone with my brother. He had a talk with Clark tonight. Told him he wasn't welcome at our Sunday dinners anymore."

"Oh? How did that go over?"

"Apparently it was a really tough conversation. Clark wants Justin and Geneva to move in with him. When he heard Justin was planning to ask Debbie-Ann to marry him, he almost went ballistic."

"Has Clark always been such a controlling father?"

"I think so. Yes. You'd have to talk to Justin to be sure."

"Has your mom decided whether to talk to Zak about the baby switching?"

"She wants to. But she's afraid to hurt Justin."

"I guess it's her call. But I hate to see that slime ball get away with what he did. Makes me wonder if he's got other skeletons in his closet, you know?"

✕

May 6

MONDAY MORNING NADINE put a box of her old western romances into the passenger side of her truck. Though it wasn't yet eight, the sun already felt warm and the mating melodies of the house finches as they cavorted in the pine trees added to her good mood.

"What are those for?" Zak came up from behind and dropped a kiss on her neck.

Nadine turned in to him. They'd spent the night together and made love. Later, instead of whispering sweet nothings, they'd talked about the case.

Nadine was a practical woman. She had important personal matters to discuss with this guy, but now was not the time.

"I promised the books to Amber. I'm going to swing by

her place after I check the properties on Loon Lake." She gave Zak a final kiss, then stepped up into the driver's seat. She had a travel mug of coffee and a lot on her mind, so the drive went quickly.

Loon Lake was a small, pristine gem located in the valley south of town. The sapphire-blue waters were fed by the melting snow off the Bitterroots. Tall rock cliffs prevented development on three sides of the lake, but the land on the south-facing shore sloped gently toward the water.

Back in the fifties and sixties that land was subdivided into half-acre lots for summer cabins. The cabins were mostly small A-frames, nestled into the forest of ponderosa pine, Douglas fir and Rocky Mountain junipers.

Twelve years ago half of those properties had been purchased and repackaged into full-acre lots with brand-new luxury cottages more than four times the square footage of the old cabins. These expensive homes, vacant for most of the year, were prime targets for break-ins and robberies, which was why someone from their department did a drive-through at least a few times a month.

Nadine drove slowly along the single dirt road that provided access to all the cottages. The newer ones had double garages and bear-proof garbage bins. In the summer, residents could pay for garbage pickup, but that didn't start until after Memorial Day.

As she cruised by the luxury homes, she thought what a shame it was that so many of them sat empty for the majority of the year. They probably had gorgeous kitchens, walk-in closets, floor-to-ceiling windows looking over the lake and mountains beyond.

The road curved gently as it followed the shore and, suddenly seeing something in her path ahead, she slowed. Garbage littered the road. Cardboard pizza boxes, plastic packaging, juice bottles and milk jugs, a real mess.

Nadine glanced at the nearby homes. It was easy to see the source of the problem. One of the bear-proof bins had been knocked over. Whoever dumped all this garbage must have neglected to close the lid properly.

She cut the engine and swung down from her truck, studied the ground around the debris and found a telltale pile of bear scat. She went to the back entry of the house and rang the doorbell.

No response. She knocked. Still nothing.

There were no windows into the garage so no way to tell if a vehicle was parked inside. Nadine circled the cottage, but all the blinds were closed. She ended up on the deck overlooking the lake. A thick layer of dust clung to the beige plastic covers over the patio furniture and barbecue.

Whoever had left their garbage bins unfastened seemed to be long gone.

She was about to head back to the road when the haunting, wistful call of a loon floated over the water. She sat on one of the steps leading down to the water and used her hand to shield the sun from her eyes. The lake was perfectly calm, reflecting back the deep blue of the sky, the wild forest at its edges.

And then she spotted the bird in the sky. The black-and-white loon dropped down quickly to the lake and began swimming toward shore. From a patch of bulrushes, another loon emerged, this one with a chick resting on its back.

Nadine held her breath. Loons were notoriously shy. And while she usually spotted a few every year, she'd never seen a mother with a baby on its back before. Too bad Zak wasn't here. He would freakin' love this.

She watched until the loons were nothing but specks on the blue, then got up and brushed the dust from her trousers.

Back to work.

She put on a pair of gloves, then stuffed the trash back into the bin, this time making sure the lid was properly fastened. Stinky work—the garbage was fresh, probably the culprits had been down for the weekend.

Funny they hadn't taken the covers off their furniture then. But maybe it had been too cool to sit out on the deck.

Back in her truck, she drove to the far end of the road, then looped back the way she'd come. Nothing else was amiss. Hopefully the bear, wherever he was, would move on now that there was no more garbage to tempt him.

IT WAS ALMOST noon when Nadine reached the Woodrows'

farm. Amber wasn't out in the garden—maybe she was inside having lunch. Nadine drove past the maple trees and parked next to the house. She was greeted by the lazy, old Lab, who wagged his tail when she scratched his neck.

She grabbed the box of books and went to the back door.

A thicket of raspberries grew behind the house. Next to that, sheets flapped on a clothesline. From the other side of the screen door she could hear Carrie Underwood singing "Love Wins."

Nadine set the books down so she could knock.

Amber appeared on the other side of the screen, stuffing her arms into a baggy plaid shirt. "Oh. Hi." Once the shirt was on, she opened the door. Her gaze dropped to the box of books. "Wow."

"I promised you some books." The sleeves of Amber's shirt were rolled up a few inches so Nadine could see her wrists. The bruises were still there, but fainter.

"Oh gosh, that's so nice of you." Amber's eyes had the puffy look of someone who'd been crying. She dabbed at a bit of moisture trailing down her cheek. "Dang allergies. Come on in. I'll turn down the music."

Nadine dropped the box onto a kitchen chair while Amber made some adjustments on her phone, until you could hardly hear the music at all. Then the young woman glanced inside the box. "Fantastic. This will last me all summer."

"Good. I hope you enjoy them."

Amber had been making sandwiches. Slices of bread,

beef and cheese were spread out on the counter.

"I really appreciate the books. Especially since the library might be closed all summer."

"Why do you say that?"

"Well, Dad, he said people in town are talking that way. Like something really bad must have happened to Ms. Tombe."

Amber looked as if she wanted Nadine to say something to dispute that. Unfortunately, she couldn't.

"We're still actively investigating the case." But for how much longer would that be true? As she and Zak had discussed last night, they were running out of leads to follow.

"That's good." Amber didn't sound too hopeful. "Anyway, thanks for the books. Would you like a sandwich and some lemonade?"

Nadine could see there was enough food for two people, but presumably one of these sandwiches was meant for Amber's dad. "That's okay. I should be on my way." She was turning away when she noticed a wad of tissues on the kitchen counter.

"Listen, Amber, my boyfriend told me what happened to your mom. I'm so sorry. If I can do anything to help, you'll let me know, right?" Her gaze dropped to Amber's wrists. "I mean, if your dad's drinking—"

The sound of heavy work boots on the back stoop startled Nadine, and Amber too. The screen door opened, and a tall, heavyset man dressed in work clothes walked in. On his head was a John Deere cap. His face was lined and weathered and grimy. But he had the same deep-set eyes as his daughter.

His gaze traveled from Nadine to his daughter, then back again. "What's the law doing way out here?"

"I just dropped some books off for your daughter." Nadine couldn't tell if Amber was scared of her father, or just indifferent. His appearance certainly hadn't brought a smile.

"Lunch is almost ready, Dad. I'll put on some coffee."

When the older man didn't respond, Nadine offered her hand. "I'm Deputy Nadine Black."

"Pete Woodrow."

His skin felt like sandpaper, his grip like a vice.

"How'd you come to know my daughter?"

"Nadine was a barrel racer, Dad. Mom and I saw her compete in Missoula."

"Is that where you met?"

The man was a bulldog. He would not be distracted.

"I was driving by last week and saw Amber in the garden. I stopped to ask for some water, and we got to talking. I found out we have similar taste in books, so…" Nadine glanced at the box of paperbacks.

Pete did not look impressed. "Amber has plenty to keep her busy here on the farm without reading that trash. From now on, why don't you mind your own business, Deputy?"

Nadine glanced at Amber, to see how she felt about this. But Amber was making coffee, her back turned to both of them.

“In other words, I’d thank you to leave my property. Now.”

“I’m going.” On her way to the door Nadine held Pete’s gaze, wanting him to get the message that she might be leaving, but she was not intimidated. Before closing the door, she said good-bye to Amber.

The young woman did not respond.

Nadine hated to leave. She was afraid Amber was going to get yelled at, maybe even knocked around, by her father. She sat for a while in her truck with her window open, alert for signs of conflict.

But there was only silence. Eventually the country music started playing again. Nadine drove off.

Chapter Fifteen

When Sheriff Ford had been in charge, the office wall across from the windows had displayed his hunting trophies. The mounted whitetail buck and big-horned sheep had been packed up with the rest of Ford's belongings during the transition period and Zak had them replaced with a massive whiteboard and a topo map of the county. He was standing in front of the whiteboard now, black marker in hand.

He'd spent the past hour writing down all the known facts about Sybil's abduction, as well as a list of possible persons of interest. Here was the big picture. What was he missing?

The main door opened and banged shut. Through his partially open office door he heard Nadine check in with Bea and then snatches of their exchange. A bear getting into garbage at a cottage on Loon Lake. Some conversation about Amber Woodrow. Had Bea known Amber's mother?

And then his door flew open and Nadine breezed in carrying...a bowl of apples?

She set the bowl on an empty corner of his desk. "Figured it was time we had some healthy food around for snacking. I put another bowl next to the coffee machine."

"Not a bad idea."

"Sorry I'm late for the meeting." She glanced around. "Where's Kenny?"

"He won't be back for another thirty minutes. I asked him to patrol the school and day care during lunch hour. I'm hoping he spots that old guy who's been ogling the kiddies and brings him in for questioning."

"As if we don't have enough problems. You think the geezer means any harm?" Nadine settled into a chair with a view of the whiteboard.

"Let's hope not. We'll see what Kenny has to report. Meanwhile, let's review the case, differentiating between known facts and inferences."

Nadine turned her attention to the board. "Known fact number one: Last sighting of Sybil was at the Natural Grocers store shortly after six."

"Correct. We know she went home after that, because her groceries were on the floor at the front door, with the dated and time-stamped receipt."

"We also know a cowboy-hat-wearing man with a beard, driving a dark, muddy pickup truck with all-season tires was seen in her driveway around three o'clock."

"The spare key to Sybil's house was missing—that's a fact. We believe our bearded man used the key to gain access to her home—that's an educated guess."

"Hey, are you the only one allowed to have a marker?"

He tossed her a second dry-erase marker.

"The shattered glass and spilled vegetable juice are a fact." Nadine went to the board and numbered the fact.

"Yes. Based on that, we've inferred that Sybil was startled in the kitchen by something. Possibly the bearded man." He studied the board. "There was no evidence of a struggle, no blood, no furniture out of place. Sybil could have left with the man willingly—maybe she knew him."

"But then wouldn't she have taken her purse and cell phone? And maybe she was in a rush then, but an hour or two later, or even the next morning, she would have called a friend or neighbor and asked them to put a note on the library door."

"You're right. I think it's safe to infer she didn't leave willingly, but was somehow overpowered and made to get into that truck."

Nadine nodded. "I agree. We know he didn't shoot her, or stab her, or hurt her in any way that would have caused severe bleeding. So is it safe to assume she was alive at that point?"

"There are other ways of ending a life—strangulation for one. But we'll proceed on the hope that Sybil is still living until we have evidence otherwise."

"If only we had some idea about motive. We don't even know if this was a random thing or if Sybil was specifically targeted."

"We have that anonymous letter you found at her desk in the library," Zak reminded her. "We won't know if it was sent by the same guy until we get the handwriting analysis. But if it was, it suggests this guy knew her. And targeted her."

Nadine gave him an impressed look. He loved when she did that. She made him feel smart. Probably smarter than he really was.

"Reasons being?"

"Could be sexual in nature. Could be he wanted some sort of revenge after being rejected."

"Which brings us to the guys from Montana Matches. Do we have any other possible candidates?"

"None. Aside from attending college, Sybil lived her entire life in Lost Trail. Kenny's followed up with all her friends, colleagues and neighbors—he's checked everyone on the contact list on her phone—and we haven't come up with a single person of interest or lead to follow."

"Okay. So we're back to our three guys from Montana Matches."

"Exactly. Let's consider them." Zak had made a chart on the board earlier. Suspects on the top, then on the right-hand side four columns: Beard, Tires, Alibi.

"Number one, Jeffery Taylor," Zak continued. "He had a beard—well a goatee—and his truck had all-season tires. Plus, he had no alibi from eleven Thursday afternoon onward."

"Which brings us to number two, Dr. Zane Elser." Nadine underscored his name. Clearly, she enjoyed using that marker. "Elser has a beard, so that's a check. But his truck tires had winter treads with studs... Could he have borrowed or rented another vehicle?"

"If he did, maybe he got the same person to agree to save his document every fifteen minutes to provide his alibi. It seems that both Elser and Thomson would have needed an accomplice. In Thomson's case I know who that accomplice would be."

Zak wrote the name "Rick Wright" beside Martin Thomson's name. "Rick has the beard and the truck with the all-season tires, while Marty is the one with the motive. The only alibi they have is for Thursday at six was provided by each other."

Bea entered the room, surveyed the whiteboard. "Impressive. Does all this writing have a solution?"

"Not yet," Zak hated to admit.

"Well, maybe things will be clearer when those lab results come in. I gave them a call like you asked. They've put a rush on checking those tire impressions. And the handwriting analysis."

"Thanks, Bea."

"In the meantime, we've got more problems. Debbie-Ann just called. She and her assistant were taking the kiddies to the park for a spring treasure hunt when she noticed an older man sitting on a park bench, watching them. She said he didn't do or say anything threatening, but given what happened to Darby Larkin last week, Debbie-Ann decided to abort her plans and take the kids back to the day care."

Zak could tell Bea was worried. So was he. "Okay. Get Kenny to head over to the park STAT and see if he can spot that man."

"I called him right after I spoke with Debbie-Ann and he's on it. When he's finished checking the park, he'll get a statement from Debbie-Ann."

"I'll meet him over there," Zak decided. He turned to Nadine. "Maybe the geezer saw Kenny's vehicle patrolling the school and the day care and that was why he decided to hang out at the park."

NOT A SINGLE vehicle was parked in Lost Trail Park's graveled lot. Seemed like a shame. The day was a sunny gift from the climate change gods—not too hot, not too cold, in other words, perfect. The new grass and leaves were so green they sparkled, and the cheery clumps of arrowleaf balsamroot flowers were abundant.

Zak made a slow sweep of the lot. Not a child was on the playground equipment. The cedar benches were vacant too. In the northwest corner of the park was the entrance to his favorite running trail. It led to the peak of Strawberry Mountain, for those inclined.

Today, no one seemed inclined.

Next Zak drove to the Little Cow Pokes Day Care.

He remembered the day Debbie-Ann had opened her new business. He'd still been working at his father's hardware store—before his grandfather died and left his folks the farm in South Dakota—and Debbie-Ann had come in to buy a sheet of plywood and some stencils to make a sign.

The sign was still up there, hanging off the front porch railing where she'd nailed it. She must varnish it every year because the letters, painted in bright primary colors, were as fresh as ever.

Zak parked behind Kenny's vehicle. It was a bit past two, so parents wouldn't be coming to pick up their children for a while. He ran up the stairs to the porch and peered in the glass pane of the front door. The kids were sitting on pieces of carpet, listening as a redheaded young woman read them a story.

He didn't know the girl but judging by her hair color guessed she was the daughter of the woman who owned the Natural Grocers store, Elaine Cobbles.

On the other side of the room, his deputy and Debbie-Ann had their backs to the children and were in deep conversation. Zak wedged open the door and Debbie-Ann waved him over.

"Hey, Zak, I'm just about finished getting her statement."

Kenny didn't look annoyed that his boss was butting in

on him. It was so refreshing when adults behaved like adults.

"Good work." He focused on Debbie-Ann. He'd always liked her smile. There was a sweetness about it. Right now, though, she was chewing on her bottom lip and her forehead was creased with anxiety.

"Zak, there was something about this guy. He scared me."

"Did you recognize him?" Like him, Debbie-Ann was born and raised here. Between them they must know almost everyone in the county.

"No. I'm sure I've never seen him before. I wouldn't have forgotten him. His eyes…" She shivered. "I was too far away to see the color, but he was watching the children so intensely."

"Any child in particular?"

Debbie-Ann swallowed, and her hands went to her heart. "I think it was Ashley."

Zak had noticed the taller child amid the smaller ones. "Why isn't she at school today?"

"I heard what happened to Darby Larkin on Friday. Justin thought I was crazy, but I insisted on keeping both Ashley and Geneva with me today."

Both Ashley and Darby were slender girls with long, light-colored hair. Was that the profile this guy was after?

"To tell you the truth," Debbie-Ann went on, "I haven't felt safe since Sybil disappeared. She's the closest I've had to a mother since my grams died. When Ashley was a baby, I'd sometimes leave her with Sybil at the library for an hour or two so I could run errands or grab a nap. And Sybil's so great with my day care kids. They love her story hour. I can't imagine this town or my life without her."

"We are following every possible lead trying to find her," Zak said.

"And we're also keeping a close eye out for this man you saw today," Kenny added.

Zak nodded. He wished they had more to offer in terms of reassurance. Back when he'd been working for Sheriff Ford it had been so easy to criticize the older man. But now Zak understood the enormity of the pressure that came with this job.

The safety of all the children, the ones in this room, and every child in the county, was his responsibility. His.

"YOU SEEM TENSE." Nadine slipped her arm around Zak's waist. "I'm guessing this isn't a good time to talk about visiting my parents."

He pulled her closer. They were outside the paddock, watching the sun slip behind the Bitterroots. The end of another long—both literally and figuratively—day.

He'd clocked fourteen hours today. Yet felt guilty about stepping away from the job.

"Let's talk about our day first. You haven't told me about

your visit to Amber Woodrow's. Did she like the books?"

"Yes, but her father didn't. He came in for lunch shortly after I arrived and practically kicked me out the door. Are you sure he was a nice man before his wife died?"

"Guilt can really eat at a person."

"To the point where their own children are afraid of them?"

"You sure Amber is afraid of him?"

"Either afraid or indifferent. And what about those bruises on her wrists?"

"Maybe she got them some other way."

"That girl is terrified, Zak. I see it in her eyes. I wish I'd had a chance to talk to her longer. See if I could get her to open up."

"You know what I'd do if you're really concerned? Talk to Gertie."

"The lady who works at the convenience store?"

Slowly but surely Nadine was learning the who's who of their town. "None other. If there are any rumors floating around town, she'll have heard them."

"I'll do that."

Nadine sounded relieved to have a plan. She was genuinely worried about Amber, which made Zak wonder if he should be more concerned than he was. He was about to ask for more details about the girl, when Nadine gave an excited, "Oh!"

She pulled her phone out of her back pocket. "I forgot to

show you these pictures I took at Loon Lake this morning. Isn't this amazing?"

He expected to see a garbage bin demolished by a bear. Instead she showed him a female loon with a baby riding on her back. He whistled. "That's awesome." He scrolled through the series of pictures, amazed at how clear the images were.

When he finished, he handed the phone back and realized Nadine had been watching him, not the camera.

"I love that you're a bird geek."

"Most women do find it an irresistible quality."

Chapter Sixteen

ZAK WENT TO bed with Nadine, slept a few hours, then was awake at three. Nadine had her back to him. Out cold.

Quietly he eased from under the down comforter, planting his feet on the cold plank flooring. He grabbed his clothing from the chair next to the door and got dressed in the bathroom. If he couldn't sleep, he might as well go home and keep his cat company. This living part-time at home and part-time at Nadine's was beginning to get old. He wondered if she ever thought of moving in together. He was reluctant to bring the subject up, since obviously it would be her house they'd end up in, because horses were rarely permitted in basement suites.

Watson put on a show of not caring less that his so-called master was home. He didn't even bother to come out of whatever hiding space he'd found until after Zak had settled on the sofa with a mug of instant cocoa he'd made in the microwave.

If this was an old-time western, and he was playing the part of a stymied sheriff, Zak had no doubt he'd be drinking bourbon. But any man who grew up with an alcoholic father either became an alcoholic himself or set stringent rules around alcohol consumption.

And for Zak, drinking alone was a very rare thing.

He drank his cocoa and wondered what the hell he was missing.

Focusing on the men Sybil had met on the online dating site seemed a no-brainer. There was nothing else going on in her life at Lost Trail that raised alarm bells.

Everyone loved and valued her.

No one they'd interviewed had been able to name a single person who might wish her harm.

But obviously there was such a person. Was it possible the same man was skulking around town, targeting children? The only thing connecting the two was the facial hair, the man's age, and a cowboy hat.

In a small county like this one, though, it was difficult to believe two serious crimes could be going on at the same time and not be connected.

He wished Debbie-Ann had taken a picture of the man in the park today. From her description in the detailed statement she'd given Kenny, the man might have been either Rick Wright (in cahoots with Marty Thomson) or Dr. Zane Elser. But how did it make sense to abduct a woman past middle age and then go after a prepubescent girl?

May 7

TUESDAY MORNING, ZAK went back to Sybil's house. How handy if criminals really did head back to the scene of their crime. In his experience, however, this was a myth.

Using the key he'd taken from Sybil's purse, he let himself in the back door, then proceeded to tour through the rooms. He took his time, hoping to see something he'd missed in the adrenaline-fueled first days after Sybil's disappearance.

The house had been vacant for less than a week, but already it felt colder, cheerless, neglected. Not even Sybil's bright pillows and colorful artwork could alter the air of despondency in the place.

Or maybe the despondency was coming from him, seeping out of his pores, as he considered the dreadful possibility that he wasn't a better sheriff than Archie Ford. Maybe, in fact, he was worse.

What was he missing?

Zak looked through the items in Sybil's bathroom vanity and her bedside table. All confirmed that Sybil was the woman she appeared to be. A commonsense woman who believed in good grooming, but nothing more. There was toothpaste and dental floss, cleansing creams and moisturizers.

There was no exotic perfume or expensive cosmetics. No erotic literature or sex toys.

In her office he found Sybil's financial records, which

confirmed what Tiff had told them. Sybil wasn't rich, but she was comfortably well-off. They'd already been in touch with her bank. So far, her assets hadn't been touched since she'd disappeared. And the pattern of her deposits and withdrawals in the past six months was totally normal. All of which seemed to rule out a financial motive for her disappearance.

Zak returned to the kitchen. Once more the stuffed teddy bear called out to him. He studied it closely and noticed the fur was matted and rubbed bare in places. He pulled out an evidence bag and gloves and tagged the bear as evidence.

Evidence of what, he wasn't sure.

Snuggling?

TUESDAY MORNING, ONE hour after Justin had dropped Debbie-Ann at the day care and the girls at school—where he'd waited until they were safely inside—his sister called him.

"Sorry to phone you at work," Tiff said, "but I didn't want Geneva overhearing any part of this conversation."

"Sounds serious." Justin saved the document he'd been working on, then closed the door between himself and his receptionist Gwen.

"What's up?"

"Do you remember the day you and your dad told us

about the baby switching?"

He sank back into his chair. "Like I'll ever forget that."

"Your father had a sealed envelope. He claimed it contained his signed confession."

"Yeah…?" He didn't like the sound of this.

"What happened to that letter?"

"I don't know."

"Did you ever read it?"

"No. Clark said it was a confession letter." But for all he knew, Clark Pittman had stuck a blank piece of paper in that envelope. "Mom really wants him to go to jail, doesn't she?"

"She's still thinking about it. She doesn't want to hurt you, Justin. But I do think it would be good to have the letter. If it hasn't been destroyed."

Justin didn't want to deny Rosemary and Tiffany anything. They'd suffered so much more than him. Casey's illness and death followed quickly by Irving's fatal accident—which hadn't really been an accident. Then there were the years Marsha had tried to hide her shameful crimes by secretly drugging Rosemary.

His father had played a role in all of that.

"I don't know what happened to the letter. Clark may have destroyed it."

"I realize that. But could you look? You must know where he keeps his most important papers."

Justin did know. There was a fireproof safe in his father's home office.

"I need to think about this."

Tiff was silent. He guessed she wasn't pleased. Then he heard her sigh.

"He's a criminal, Justin," she said softly. Then she hung up.

THIRTY MINUTES LATER Justin's cell phone rang again. Debbie-Ann's picture showed on the display. She never called him at work unless it was important, so he grabbed it.

"Hey there. You okay?"

"I'm safe. The girls are fine. But I'd really like to talk to you. Can you get away for a few minutes?"

"I'll be right there."

Whatever was going on in this town was getting to her. Was getting to all of them.

Justin asked Gwen to explain to his next client that he might be a few minutes late.

"Where are you going?"

"To the day care. I shouldn't be long." He walked out in his shirtsleeves having left his jacket hanging on the back of his chair. The day care was only a few blocks away. When he arrived, the children were at tables working with clay. He watched through the glass panel at the top of the door as Lori and Debbie-Ann moved from child to child, offering praise or assistance as required.

He'd convinced Debbie-Ann to let their girls go to school today. With the fenced school yard, Kenny Bombard doing regular patrols, and the school staff on high alert, he felt Ashley and Geneva were safer at school than anywhere else.

He hoped nothing had happened to make him regret that decision.

Finally, Debbie-Ann glanced in his direction and he waved a hand for her to come outside. If she was upset, it was best they spoke where no little ears could possibly hear.

"Justin. Thank you for coming." She tucked her hair behind her ears and a piece of clay fell onto her shoulder. He picked it up and flicked it to the lawn.

"Looks nice and normal in there. What's wrong?"

"What's wrong is your father came by about half an hour ago, demanding to speak to me in private."

Justin's muscles tightened.

"He told me that you didn't really love me, that I was just a convenient woman who happened to be in the right place at the right time." Debbie-Ann's gaze slid to the wooden porch floor. Her voice quietened. "He said I wasn't smart enough or beautiful enough for you."

"What bullshit." Justin took Debbie-Ann's hands. They felt clammy and cool. He didn't like the way she was avoiding his gaze. "I hope you told him to go to hell."

"He said more, Justin. That you felt you owed me after the way I helped out when you were sick."

She'd raised her gaze a little, but only to the level of his chin. He gently cupped the sides of her face and stooped a little, until his eyes were level with hers. "You're not buying that crap?"

She still wouldn't look at him.

"He made me feel like I was taking advantage of you and the fact that you'd been so ill for so long."

The dirty old fox. He hadn't been able to convince Justin to move in, so now he was trying to sabotage Justin's relationship with Debbie-Ann. He gritted his teeth. Fiery anger flared, clouding his brain. He closed his eyes, sucked in a slow, deep breath. *Bastard.* "He's lying. He's trying to drive a wedge between us."

"He's your father. I'm sure he wants the best for you. So why would he try to drive away a woman you really loved?"

"Good question."

But the picture was finally coming into focus. He'd been a pawn. So freaking easy to manipulate. But no more.

"I don't think Clark ever had my best interests in mind in anything he did. He sure didn't today when he said all those awful things to you. Please don't believe them. He already robbed me of growing up with my real parents and my sister. Don't let him take away the woman I love as well, just so he can get what he wants."

And what Clark wanted, what Clark had always wanted, was to control Justin, the son he stole from another family.

AT NINE THIRTY Nadine walked up and down the aisles in the convenience store, looking for something at least moderately healthy to eat. Usually she could count on Zak cooking her nutritious things like grilled salmon, with big crunchy salads and lots of roasted vegetables. Then in the morning he'd make her green smoothies and real oatmeal, the kind you cooked in a pot.

But just when she needed him most, Zak had been losing his healthy habits. He was going for the fast food way too often. She couldn't even remember the last time he'd been on a run, let alone coaxed her along.

Being sheriff was a tough gig.

Finally, she settled on a package of roasted peanuts. She took it to the counter.

Gertie Humphrey was crouched over a bowl on the floor, filling it with kibble. Only then did Nadine notice a mid-sized white dog with a mostly black face, sleeping on a large, padded dog bed.

"This is Alfred," Gertie said. "Took him for a long walk this morning. He'll be happy to sleep for the rest of the morning."

"Must be nice to bring your pet to work with you." She could imagine the chaos if she dared bring Junior to the office. But maybe in a few years once he'd gotten his puppyhood out of his system.

Gertie rang up the peanuts with thin hands, fingers wizened by arthritis. Nadine had to remember to ask Zak how old Gertie was. Judging by her hair and hands she was eighty. But the keen light in her pale blue eyes spoke of a much younger spirit.

"Hear you're working hard at the sheriff's office these days."

"We are," Nadine agreed.

"Hope you get to the bottom of it soon. Sybil's been gone for five days."

As if she hadn't felt the passage of each hour of those five days like a noose tightening at her neck. "We're working on it. Following up every lead we've got."

"And what about that pervert hanging around the kiddies? We're getting the nicest weather we've had since last fall and parents are scared to take their children to the park."

"It's a worry. But we're doing extra patrols, watching out for him. Citizens can help by calling the office immediately if they notice anyone suspicious loitering around."

"Don't worry about me. If I see someone up to no good, I'll call all right." Gertie handed over the peanuts and Nadine's change. "Now was there anything else you wanted to ask me?"

Nadine drew back, eyebrows raised.

"Law enforcement comes in to buy something when they aren't getting gas...well, they're usually wanting some information."

"You're saying I didn't need to buy the peanuts." Nadine snapped her fingers with faked regret.

"The protein will be good for you." Gertie leaned her elbows on the counter. "Now what is it you want to ask?"

"Amber Woodrow. Do you know her?"

"Amber. Oh my. I haven't seen her in ages. She dropped out of school after her mother died in that awful farming accident. You heard about that?"

Nadine lowered her gaze to the counter. "I did."

A few seconds went by. Gertie cleared her throat. "Then you know what that family's been through. No one blames Amber's brother for leaving Lost Trail. But it's a shame he left Amber alone in that house. Pete isn't coping very well from what I hear."

"Do you think Amber's in any danger from her father?"

Gertie's posture stiffened. "Heavens no. Pete may be drinking too much, and shutting himself off from his friends and neighbors, but he would never hurt his daughter. But why are you asking about the Woodrows?"

Nadine got the implied criticism. Shouldn't all their efforts be focused on finding Sybil? "I drove by their farm when I was out on patrol Friday morning." In other words, before anyone knew Sybil was missing. "Amber was working in the garden and I stopped to talk to her. I got the impression that she was very unhappy."

"She lost her mother. Of course, she's unhappy." Gertie relaxed a little. "You're new to Lost Trail, but I've known

Pete and Iris forever. Good solid people. Pete will sort himself out eventually. And Amber, well, she'll be fine too."

Nadine thought about the bruises. The way Amber had seemed to shrink when her father entered the kitchen.

Gertie might have her finger on the pulse of Lost Trail. But this time she might be getting the wrong reading.

✕

TWO HOURS LATER, Justin still wanted to punch something. Seething about the things his father had said to Debbie-Ann, he slammed a hand on his desk, pulled up from his chair, and then paced.

Ever since Franny had died when Justin was only six, his father had said it was the two of them against the world.

But it hadn't been true. Justin had another family. And Tiff was right, it was time he stood up for them.

There was a tap on his door. Gwen peeked in. As usual she was in heels and a dress, hair styled and face made up. He'd told her "dressy casual" when he hired her, but she was always turned out like an extra on a big-city legal drama.

"I'm going to grab a sandwich at the Snowdrift. Can I get you anything?"

"I'm not hungry. Thanks though."

"Not hungry? Sounded like you were running a marathon in here."

"Tricky legal problem. I think best when I'm moving."

"Right." She raised an eyebrow.

"Take your keys. I may be out when you get back."

"Oh? Where?"

He waved his hand. "Just give me a call if something comes up."

Gwen put a hand on her hip and gave him a look. She wasn't one of those discreet receptionists who took orders and kept quiet. She wanted to be in the loop.

But not this time. He gave her a smile and said nothing more, until she finally shrugged and left.

Justin kept a set of his father's house keys at his office. He grabbed them, then left the office, locking the door behind him. He raced down the stairs, past the sound of the dentist's drill on the main floor, and then out to the street.

The beautiful weather seemed to be in a welcome holding pattern over their corner of the world. Justin headed west, nodding hello to a rancher on the other side of the street whose will he'd drawn up last month. The man was in a tricky situation where one son wanted to stay on the land and continue the family cattle operation, while the other was pursuing a real estate career in Missoula. How to be fair to both of them, yet not strip so much financially from the ranch that it wasn't sustainable.

Justin had come up with an elegant solution involving incorporation with voting and nonvoting shares that had satisfied the entire family.

Though he'd started his practice in Lost Trail to make

his father happy, Justin didn't totally regret the decision. It was satisfying working for people who were your neighbors and friends. He knew Debbie-Ann felt the same way. After her grandmother died, she could have sold the family house and moved to a city to start a new life.

Instead she'd opted to stay and open her own business and build her life here.

Their commitment to this town and this community was partly why they were such a good fit. But his dad's suggestion that Justin wanted to marry Debbie-Ann because the union was convenient or because he was settling was dead wrong.

Justin loved her. His emotions were all the more powerful for the deep roots of friendship that they had grown from. Finding that confession for Tiff and his mother would have the added benefit of proving to Debbie-Ann just where his loyalties lay.

Driftwood Road dead-ended at Lost Creek. To the right was the park, to the left the enclave of estate homes, of which his father's home was one. Justin knew who lived in every one of these homes. There was the house Derick Sparks had moved into with Aubrey after they were married. Following a separation of almost two years, the couple was together again, raising their adopted son Brody.

When Justin reached his father's home, he tried the bell first. When there was no answer, he let himself inside, then went to the door that connected to the garage. His father's sedan was gone.

Off on another of his so-called "aimless drives in the country"? Justin suddenly didn't buy it. His father didn't do anything aimlessly.

On the kitchen counter he saw a couple real estate listings, one for a hobby farm ten miles north from town, the other for a larger piece of land to the west. Justin studied the sheets for a few moments. Both pieces of property showed beautiful homes. One had a small barn with an attached paddock. Suddenly it hit him. Clark was looking at buying something for the three of them: Clark, Justin and Geneva.

Justin ripped the Realtor's business card from the top of one of the listings. No doubt Clark figured once he owned the property, Justin would cave to his demands. Why wouldn't he think that? Justin had a history of doing exactly what his father wanted him to do.

He went directly to his father's study, to the safe in the cabinet under the bookshelf. As his father's executor, he knew the combination. He turned the combination this way, then the other, back again. And the door opened.

Inside was a substantial stack of manila envelopes. He recognized the one that had been prepared in his office—his father's will. There were also legal papers regarding the house, Franny's death certificate, a packet of insurance information…

Methodically Justin went through all the envelopes, until finally he came upon a single white business envelope on which was written: *For Justin after my death.*

For a long moment he examined the envelope. This had to be it. The confession. He folded the envelope in half and stuffed it in his pocket.

Chapter Seventeen

"JEFFERY TAYLOR'S HERE to see you, Zak."

The time on Zak's computer was ten minutes past five. Where had the day gone? He got up from his desk and pulled a screen down over the whiteboard. "Thanks, Bea, send him in."

Though he didn't often wield his power officiously, Zak judged this would be a good time to position himself behind his desk. Jeffery Taylor came in like a man on a mission, worried, determined, intense.

"Welcome to Lost Trail, Mr. Taylor. What can I do for you?"

"She's been gone five days, Sheriff. I want to know what's being done to find her."

Zak nodded. "Sit down. Would you like some coffee?"

Taylor shook his head. With his neatly trimmed goatee, black Harry Potter eyeglasses, gray slacks and button-down blue shirt, he looked the epitome of an academic. Zak felt an instant affinity for the man. He seemed like the perfect match for Sybil.

But people weren't always how they appeared.

"We've been putting most of our resources into this case, Mr. Taylor. And we are following up several leads. But I'd welcome any input you can offer. I've read the statement you gave Deputy Bombard. Have you got anything to add? Maybe you've remembered a detail that didn't seem important at the time?"

"I told your deputy everything I could think of. Sybil and I have been seeing each other around a month. We covered our basic histories on our first date—where we were born, how many siblings, where we went to college, that sort of thing. I told her about my first wife, but we didn't dwell on that stuff. Mostly we discussed books and movies and current affairs."

"Did she ever tell you that May was a difficult month for her?"

"Why yes," Taylor lifted his head in interest. "Now that you mention it."

"Did she tell you why?"

"She said she lost someone very important to her at that time of year. I didn't ask who. I figured when she was ready, she would tell me."

Zak thought of the calendar. Nadine had taken a photograph of May and he'd seen for himself all the little black hearts Sybil had drawn in the square for May fifth. He made a note to check on the dates her parents and grandparents had died. From conversations he'd had with her in the past, he knew she'd been especially fond of her grandmother.

It was hard to see how this could be connected to her disappearance, but they had so little to go on, they needed to pull on each strand.

"Did you ever send Sybil a letter?"

"No. All our communication was through Montana Matches or our phones. I'm old-fashioned enough that I actually prefer to speak to people if possible."

Which might explain why he'd taken the time to drive all this way to meet with Zak. But communication worked two ways and this was Zak's chance to see if Taylor knew more than he'd let on so far.

"Did Sybil tell you she received an anonymous letter on Thursday?"

Taylor frowned. "No. She couldn't have. The last time I communicated with her was by phone Wednesday evening, around nine." Taylor cleared his throat. "Do you think the letter is important?"

"At this point we're not sure." Zak struggled to keep his own frustration out of his voice. "Frankly we don't have a lot to go on. I'd like to ask you to think hard, really hard, about your conversations with Sybil, especially in the past week or so. Was there anything she said or did that could explain her disappearance?"

"I want to help, but there's nothing, Sheriff." Taylor studied his hands for a long moment, then looked Zak in the eyes. "One of the questions I asked Sybil on our first date was why she decided to spend her career in Lost Trail rather than at a major library in a big city. You know what she said? She felt safe here."

Zak sighed. "I get the irony."

Taylor leaned forward, planting his palms on Zak's desk. "So how did it happen, Sheriff? How could she disappear from her own home?"

Zak had never felt more impotent. "I don't know. All I can promise is we won't give up until we find her."

Jeffery Taylor nodded. Moisture had pooled in his eyes. Discreetly he turned his head.

Zak did not believe he was looking at a guilty man. He was looking at a heartbroken one.

✕

AFTER LEAVING HIS father's house, Justin canceled his afternoon meetings, sent Gwen home early, and arranged for Debbie-Ann to babysit Geneva. Clark's verbal attack on Debbie-Ann had been the last straw. He needed to deal with the situation. Several options were available, including the one his mother had suggested—involving the sheriff.

But even now Justin was loath to begin a process that could end with Clark in prison.

He called his mother with another idea. Rosemary agreed it was an acceptable alternative and that she and Tiff would come to his office right away. Next he phoned Clark, who didn't hesitate when Justin asked if he could come to his office at six. Justin didn't mention Rosemary and Tiff would be there too.

The Mastersons arrived at quarter to six as he'd requested. Justin outlined the approach he planned to take and then they spent the next ten minutes perched stiffly in their chairs. Waiting.

Seconds ticked by. Minutes. Justin watched from the window anxiously until he spotted his father's car.

"He's here."

Faint sound of footsteps on the stairs, then the front door opened.

"Justin?" Clark's voice was upbeat as he entered the reception area.

Justin glanced at his mother. His sister. Both gave him encouraging nods. "In my office."

"It's been a while since you called me. I hope you'll let me buy you din—" At the threshold, Clark spotted Rosemary, then Tiff. He spun his gaze to Justin. "What's going on?"

Justin strode to Clark's side, clasped him on the arm and then closed the office door.

"The family wants to have a little chat," he said.

Clark looked at the women again and back to Justin. "This feels like an ambush."

"I think that's how Debbie-Ann felt when you went to talk to her today. Ambushed."

"Hey." Clark edged back into the only space available to

him—the nook by the window. "I only told her the truth."

"You may wish those awful things you said were true. But they aren't. You're trying to control my life again, and I've had it. I'm done with you, Clark. Done."

"I don't understand how you can say that. After all I've done for you?"

Justin didn't need to harden his heart. All he had to do was look at his mother, her arm linked with his sister's. Rosemary gazed at him with so much love and compassion. For Justin's sake she'd tried to forgive Clark for his crimes. But Justin understood now that he'd been asking too much of her. And of Tiff. And of himself, really.

"Yes, you've done a lot for me. But everything you did was predicated on the lie that you were my father. You raised me with this lie even knowing my real mother and father and sister were living just a few miles away, raising the son you'd given away because of his defective heart."

"I-I didn't do it for me. I did it for Franny."

"I bought that explanation…once." Justin nodded at his desk where he'd placed the letter he'd found in his father's safe. "I'm guessing the truth is in there. Should we open it and find out?"

"What?" Clark glanced at the letter, then recoiled. "How did you get that? You weren't supposed to see that. Not yet."

"You forget I know the combination to your safe. And after all the lines you've crossed with me, I'm not going to apologize for using it."

Clark glanced at the letter, then at the ladies, shifted feet, looked at Justin, and at the letter again.

Oh, he wanted that envelope. No doubt wanted to rip it to shreds. But Clark had to know if he made a move, Justin would beat him to it.

Clark settled back on his heels and shook his head slowly. "What do you want from me?"

"After all you've done, you probably deserve to go to jail. But we're here today—my mother and sister and I—to make you a deal. We won't hand this letter over to the sheriff, we won't tell Zak all we know, if you agree to leave this town and this county. For good."

Clark shook his head. "No, no, no. You don't mean that."

"I don't care where you go. You once said you wondered what it would be like to live in a city. Why don't you go visit your cousin in New York? Or you could try Arizona. A lot warmer there in winter."

Tiff and Rosemary joined Justin then, one on either side. He felt their arms slide across his back.

"I was only trying to protect the people I loved. Franny. You."

"You tell yourself that, Clark," Rosemary said. "But I don't believe it. You gave away your own flesh and blood so you'd have a healthy baby. But it was my baby, Clark. Mine. Every bad thing you've done has been out of concern for no one but yourself. Now you're asking my son for a loyalty you do not deserve."

"Take Justin's advice and leave," Tiff added. "Because Zak is a hell of a sheriff and if he gets this letter, he'll gather enough evidence so you end up in prison for the rest of your life.

ABOUT AN HOUR after Jeffery Taylor left his office, Zak received a text message from Tiffany Masterson. *I'd like to talk to you about something important. Can you come to Raven Farm?*

He messaged back that he was on his way.

Out in the bullpen only Kenny was at his desk. "Bea just went home. She said there'd been another complaint about a bear getting into garbage on Loon Lake. Want me to check into that?"

"Maybe later in the week." He did not have the luxury of worrying about a nuisance bear right now. "How did your patrols go today? Anyone suspicious hanging around the school or the day care?"

"Nope. I didn't give them much chance. Per your instructions I made myself very obvious."

"Good work. Why don't you head home now? None of us have had much rest lately."

Zak got in his sheriff-mobile and headed out of town. A few years ago, he'd flown in a search and rescue helicopter over Raven Farm. He'd been amazed at how beautiful the property looked from the air. Up close a Christmas tree was a Christmas tree, but from the air you could really see the variations in color and texture between the firs and the spruce and the pine.

Now as he crested the final hill, he got that same impression as he looked over the undulating fields. Conifers didn't shed their needles in the winter, but Zak could swear they were a richer green in the spring, especially the new growth on the tips of the branches.

The old family dog, Spade, came out to greet him when he arrived. A few moments later Tiff opened the front door. She was wearing faded jeans and a plaid shirt, hair pulled back in a ponytail.

"Hey, Zak, thanks for coming."

Zak flashbacked to the night Tiff returned to Lost Trail. He'd seen her visiting her father and Casey's grave sites. She'd been wearing a long, red wool coat, dressy leather boots, her hair styled in long waves, her face made-up. She'd looked more big-city than small-town girl, and he'd doubted if she would stay in Montana more than a few weeks.

She'd proved him wrong.

She'd stayed the course, faced up to her aunt Marsha and helped her mother through the rough times that followed. Now that she'd taken over the management of Raven Farm, he could tell she'd really come into her own.

He hoped whatever news she had to tell him wasn't going to threaten any of that.

"What's this about?"

"I need to get your opinion about something. It's tricky. Mom and Justin think one way, I think another..."

Zak's phone rang, and she broke off. "Need to get that?"

"Let me see." He glanced at the screen and tensed when he saw Patsy Larkin's name. He and Patsy weren't friends. If she was calling, this was official.

"Excuse me." He turned his back to Tiff and took a few steps. "Sheriff Waller here."

"Thank God! Zak, I'm so worried. I thought Darby was in her room doing homework, but when I called her for dinner she didn't come. Earlier she asked if she could go over to her best friend Courtney's house, but I said no, not unless there was an adult supervising. Now I have no idea where she is!"

"Have you called Courtney's parents?"

"Yes. Courtney's there. She's been home since school let out." Patsy was speaking faster, her pitch rising. "And they haven't seen Darby. They haven't seen her, Zak! If she meant to go to their place, she never got there."

"Patsy, I'll be right over. Are Chris and Trevor home?"

"No. They've gone out looking for Darby. Chris is in his truck. Trevor's on his bike. I wasn't sure if it was safe to let him go, but he's grown a lot this year. He's big as a man and strong."

"That's fine. Give me a call if they find her. I'm coming

over. Should be there in ten minutes." Zak pocketed his phone.

During his short tenure as sheriff, he'd never felt such dread.

"What's going on?" Tiff prompted him.

"I have to go to the Larkins'. Darby's missing."

"Oh no." Tiff wrapped her arms around her midsection. "We heard there was a suspicious older man hanging out at the school and the park…"

"We don't know yet that this is connected," Zak cautioned. "Maybe Darby just snuck out to play." If only. "I've got to go. Can we talk later?"

"Of course. Finding Darby is the priority. Can we help?"

"Yes. If she isn't found by the time we get to her house, Kenny will be organizing a search and rescue operation. Stay near your phones and be prepared to go out at a moment's notice."

A checklist of actions was running through Zak's mind. Hopefully they wouldn't be necessary. Maybe Darby's father had already found her. Man, he could sure use that extra deputy now.

Chapter Eighteen

ON THE DRIVE to the Larkins' home, Zak called Kenny and explained the situation. "Meet me at the Larkins' as soon as you can. But first call Nadine and Bea and let them know we have an emergency situation." He hoped Nadine had finished her chores. She wouldn't have much spare time for her animals tonight, unless they found Darby soon.

"What's the protocol in a situation like this?" Kenny asked. He'd never been involved in a missing persons' investigation involving a child.

"If Darby isn't found in the next fifteen minutes, then we're going to proceed on a worst-case scenario. We'll put out an Amber Alert and you'll need to mobilize search and rescue."

"Got it."

During his years as a mountain guide, Kenny had been involved in several search and rescue operations, so shortly after Zak hired him, he'd put him in charge of the county's search and rescue association. This would be his first big test.

Zak turned onto Second Street. The Larkin home was

down a block. Like Sybil's home it backed onto the forest that surrounded Lost Creek Park. A group of neighbors had gathered on Patsy's porch. She stood amidst them, but when she spotted his vehicle, she came running, almost colliding with Kenny as he jogged from the truck to the lawn.

"It must be that old guy," Patsy said. "He's got my Darby. I just know it."

The raw fear and vulnerability on Patsy's face confirmed the seriousness of the situation. No one knew her child better than Patsy. If she was this worried, there was probably cause.

But it was his job to keep her calm. "We don't know that, Patsy. Let's not jump to worst-case scenarios."

That said, he needed to conduct this investigation on that very basis. "Let's go inside so we can come up with a plan."

Keeping close to Patsy's side Zak made his way past the handful of neighbors. He nodded to those he recognized. "Thanks for your concern, folks. Deputy Bombard will be out in a few minutes to organize the search and rescue operation. If you want to help just hang around a minute and he'll tell you what to do."

Inside he followed Patsy to the kitchen. "Have you searched the house thoroughly?"

"Yes. She's not here."

"We'll go through it again, together, just to be sure." Kids were notorious for hiding, though at eight, Zak figured Darby was probably too old for this stunt. "In the meantime, do you have some recent photographs of your daughter? We'll need that for the search team."

Patsy looked at him, overwhelmed and confused. He was going too fast. He opened a few cabinets, found the glasses and poured her some water.

"Thank you."

While she drank, he checked out the room. The fridge was the stainless-steel kind. Nonmagnetic. On the opposite wall was a built-in desk. Above the desk was a corkboard and a collage of family photos. He nodded at it. "Is there a photo of Darby there?"

"Yes. Her grade three school photo."

"I'll get it."

"There should be another one from Christmas," Patsy said.

"Right." As he was pulling the tacks from the photos, Kenny arrived. "Good timing," he told his deputy. "Take these back to the office and make copies." He turned to Patsy. "Kenny's going to organize your friends and neighbors into a search party. Can you tell us what Darby is wearing today?"

"Jeans and a purple T-shirt. She's really into purple these days."

"Her shoes?"

"White sneakers."

"Good. That should be enough to start with." Zak moved closer to Kenny. "Keep me posted every thirty minutes, okay? I'm going to comb through this house with Patsy."

As Kenny turned to leave, a message sounded on Patsy's phone. She read it quickly, then groaned.

"It's Chris. He and Trevor just met at the schoolyard. They still haven't found her. They're going to head to the park."

Kenny, who'd remained to hear the outcome of the call, gave Zak a quick nod then hurried out the front door.

Zak went to sit beside Patsy. "Does Darby play in the park often?"

"No. She's not allowed in the park or the forest without an adult. Then again, neither was Trevor and he's been sneaking out since he was…around Darby's age." Patsy closed her eyes. "Oh, God," she murmured.

"Don't go thinking the worst," Zak reminded her. "Let's focus on one thing at a time. Starting with the house. Does Darby have favorite places she hides when she's upset?"

"When she was little she'd always go to her brother's closet. But that was years ago."

"Let's check it out. Just to be sure."

Trevor's room was a mess, but Patsy didn't waste time apologizing. They checked the closet and under the bed, but no luck.

They worked their way through every room in the house leaving Darby's bedroom for last. It was neater than her brother's, but not by much. From the doorway Zak eyed the collection of posters on the walls. "I see she likes puppies."

"She wants to be a vet when she grows up. She's been after us for years to buy a dog. But with our busy lifestyles, there's just no way." Tears welled in Patsy's eyes as she glanced around her daughter's room.

"The window," Zak asked. It looked out to the backyard and the forest beyond. "Was it open all day?"

"I'm not sure. It shouldn't be open at all. Chris was going to put the screens in this weekend. We haven't opened our windows since last fall when Chris and I painted."

Zak put out his arm to stop her from entering the room and closing it. "Leave everything the way it is, Patsy. We don't want to mess up anything that could be a clue to finding Darby."

"Oh God," Patsy whispered again. "Why didn't I keep her in the kitchen with me? Insist she help me make dinner, or at least do her homework at the table where I could see her?"

"This isn't your fault, Patsy. Let's go back to the kitchen and sit down at the table and then you can tell me exactly what happened."

Patsy allowed him to take her arm and lead her to the kitchen table where she sank into the same chair as earlier. Zak was about to settle next to her when the doorbell rang.

A voice called out, "Deputy Black here. Can I come in?"

Patsy's strength rallied. "Yes. We're in the kitchen."

Nadine was dressed in her regulation slacks and shirt,

hair back in a sleek ponytail. Only a piece of straw trapped in her hair betrayed the fact that she'd already gone home and done her chores.

Her gaze went straight to Zak and he pressed his lips together grimly. This was not looking good. She got the message and was all business.

"How can I help?"

"Sit down, Deputy. Patsy was just about to describe the events of the afternoon, leading up to the last time she saw her daughter. Patsy, do you need some more water?"

"No, I-I'm fine." Patsy's breath shuddered as she sucked in some air. She'd started to tremble. Nadine went to the adjoining family room, grabbed a blanket off the sofa, then wrapped it around Patsy's shoulders. Patsy pulled the edges tightly to her chest. "Where do you want me to start?"

"For now, let's focus on the afternoon. How did Darby get home from school?"

"I picked her up. Usually I take her to the Snowdrift if I'm working, but Erin Miller was there this afternoon and I trust her to close up. So Darby and I came home."

"How was her mood?"

"She was happy. Chatty. Her teacher wants them to work in pairs on a new science project and she was going to let Darby and Courtney work together. Usually they get separated because they talk too much."

"What happened after you got home?"

"I put out a snack—cookies and milk, the usual—and

then I started working on some admin stuff for the café." Patsy nodded at a pile of papers next to a laptop computer on the kitchen island. "Darby asked if she could use my iPad after her snack and I told her to get a book and do some reading instead. That's when she disappeared into her room."

Patsy's voice wobbled on the last sentence. She dropped her face into her hands and took several long, shaky breaths.

"You're doing really well," Nadine said. "Sounds like very normal mother, daughter stuff."

"It was. And then, around four thirty, our phone rang. It was Courtney asking if Darby could come over so they could plan their science project. I told Darby I didn't have time to walk her over there—Courtney lives almost a mile away. And Chris had our truck. He was at work then."

"Has Darby ever walked to Courtney's house on her own before?"

"Never. We let her play in the backyard, or with kids her age who live on this street. Those are her boundaries, and unlike her brother, Darby never challenged them."

"There's always a first time," Nadine said.

"True. But that man Darby saw last Friday—he really freaked her out. I think she would have been scared to walk to Courtney's on her own."

Zak nodded. He glanced at his watch. Thirty minutes had passed since Patsy reported her daughter missing. It was time for action.

"Patsy, could you do us a favor? Could you grab a piece of paper and write down Darby's weight and her height, as close as you can guess?" Then he took Nadine aside. "Go back to the office and put out an Amber Alert. Bea should be there by now. She can help you. We need to get word out right away."

"Definitely."

Once Nadine was gone, Zak asked Patsy to come with him to the backyard. It was easy to spot which window belonged to Darby's bedroom, as her puppy posters were clearly visible. Zak moved in closer. The paint on the window casement had been scraped away in one spot, revealing raw wood. He pointed it out to Patsy.

"You said you and Chris painted the window frames last fall?"

"Yes." Patsy looked at the spot where Zak was pointing. She clasped her hand to her mouth and turned to Zak with wide eyes, as if begging him to tell her this wasn't what it appeared.

But Zak couldn't reassure her. Not now. This was clear evidence that someone had pried Darby's window open from the outside.

"Does Darby take her shoes off when she comes into the house?"

"Yes."

"Are her shoes in the house now?"

"No. I checked for them right away. That's how I knew

she'd gone outside."

Which meant Darby hadn't left the house via the window. Perhaps whoever had pried that window open had somehow convinced Darby to put her shoes on and come outside without telling her mother.

But Darby would never have trusted the man who'd been spying on her at school. So it couldn't have happened that way.

"Zak, you're going to find her, right? Promise me, you'll find her."

Patsy was crying openly now. Zak put an arm around her shoulder, not thinking it would help, but just so she wouldn't feel alone. "I'm not going to stop till we find her, Patsy."

"I feel so helpless. I wish I could go looking for her with Chris and Trevor."

"We need you to be here, in case Darby tries to contact you. Is there someone who could come sit with you?"

"My mom."

"Good." Patsy's parents, Bonnie and Len Mitchel, lived on a ranch to the north, about twenty miles away. "Call her now."

"I already have. She and Dad are on their way. Dad's going to drop her off, then go join the search and rescue team."

Chapter Nineteen

WHEN BONNIE MITCHEL arrived, Zak led her to the kitchen where she and Patsy didn't so much hug as fall into one another's arms. "My poor baby," Bonnie murmured. "They'll find her. You have to have faith."

Zak wanted to give them space, but he didn't have the time. He cleared his throat. "We need to collect evidence from your house and yard, Patsy, so I'm going to ask you ladies to stay clear of those areas, especially the back entrance, the hallway, and Darby's room."

He waited for Patsy to nod, confirming her understanding, then went to his vehicle to grab some crime scene tape. First, he cordoned off the interior areas of the house, then ran the tape around the entire backyard.

A six-foot cedar fence separated the Larkins' home from the forest beyond. At one end of the fence, a latched gate allowed access to a walking path that connected Lost Creek Park with the ski hill. It seemed most likely that the kidnapper had gained access to Darby's bedroom via the forest.

Zak needed to get back there for a look, but he didn't want to disturb any possible fingerprints on the latch, so he went next door and accessed the forest via a neighbor's backyard.

The hiking trail was popular as an off-leash dog walking area—even at this time of year, when the risk of running into a bear, desperately hungry after winter hibernation, was higher than normal.

The dirt trail was cushioned with a thick layer of pine needles that made it feel spongy to walk along. At ground level, shrubbery, ferns and moss nestled up to the Douglas fir and ponderosa pine trees. Zak followed the path until he was behind the Larkins' house. Something yellow caught his eye. It turned out to be a ten-foot length of plastic rope tied to a mature ponderosa pine growing about five yards from the Larkins' gate.

Without touching the rope, Zak followed it to the point where it had been hacked off roughly, leaving frayed edges. He studied the ground carefully. In a few places he could see small prints in the dirt. Looked like they belonged to a dog.

Further investigation turned up some mushy dog turds, no more than a few hours old.

Zak looked back at the tree, then at the gate. This spot was exactly on line with those two points. He thought about all the puppy posters in Darby's bedroom. Such an old ruse. But effective.

He pulled his phone out of his jacket pocket and called the office.

"Hey Bea, has anyone reported a missing dog?"

"How did you know? I didn't want to bother you, but Gertie Humphrey just called. Her little terrier mix—she got him from the shelter about three weeks ago—was missing from her backyard when she got home from work."

Zak closed his eyes. How easy it had been for the kidnapper. Ridiculously easy.

He asked for a description of the dog, then said, "I expect the search and rescue people will find the dog, Bea. I'll call Kenny and tell him to keep an eye out. Meanwhile, once the Amber Alert is issued, send Nadine back here to the Larkins'. Tell her to bring the camera and evidence kit."

SHORTLY AFTER ZAK had the crime scene contained, Nadine returned. He met her on the street and waited as she left her truck and walked to his. She had a way of moving fast yet appearing calm and controlled. Zak wondered if she'd developed that skill during her years in the rodeo ring.

"Amber Alert in effect?"

She nodded. "Bulletins have already gone out on local TV and radio. Bea is putting alerts on our social media platform."

"And the FBI?"

"They're sending someone…Agent Bridge. Should be here tomorrow afternoon." Her forehead furrowed with concern. "How's Patsy holding up?"

"Her mom is here now. I've explained that we need to treat Darby's room, the backyard, and the forest behind the house as a crime scene. Come back here with me." He gestured to the walkway that led to the rear of the home. "I want to show you something."

Zak pointed out the scratches on Darby's bedroom window, then the rope and dog feces in the forest. "Get photos of everything. Dust the window frame and backyard gate for prints. We'll need that yellow cord bagged as evidence too."

"What happened here?" Nadine looked from the sawed-off cord, to Darby's window, to him.

"I'll tell you my theory later. Right now, I need to get to Gertie Humphrey's house. See if any of her neighbors saw the man who stole her dog."

"Seriously? You're checking out the missing dog now?"

"It's important." Zak phoned Kenny from his vehicle. "How's the search going?"

"Good. We have a great turnout of volunteers. I've divided them into two groups. One is going door to door in town. The other is working in sections along the creek, park and forest."

"Excellent. Keep an eye out for a white pup with black markings. Terrier mix, name on tag is Alfred. Should have the stub of a yellow rope tied to its collar. We'll want to dust the collar and the rope for prints, so try not to handle those areas unless absolutely necessary."

Lots of overgrown shrubbery surrounded the small wartime bungalow where Gertie lived. Gertie was on the weed-infested front yard in animated conversation with a woman about the same age. The other woman was taller and heavier than Gertie, with white hair cropped close to her head and large, tortoiseshell eyeglasses. Both women fell silent as Zak approached.

"Hey, Gertie. I hear you're missing a pup." He offered a hand to the other woman. "Sheriff Waller."

"Nice to meet you, Sheriff. I voted for you, but my husband stuck with Ford, so I guess we canceled each other out. I'm Denise Lang."

In different circumstances Zak might have made a joke about the voting. "Tell me what happened, Gertie."

"Since I adopted Alfred, I've been taking him to work with me. But an hour before lunch, he got into my tuna sandwiches and oatmeal cookies. Gave him the runs, so I brought him home and left him in the backyard. I figured he'd be better off there."

"Alfred didn't think so. He was yipping and crying to beat the band." Denise raised her sharp chin and pointed it at Zak. "But don't you have more important problems than a stray dog? My son was just called out by search and rescue. He told me Darby Larkin is missing."

"We think there's a connection." If Gertie normally took her dog to work, then this ploy on the part of the kidnapper had been spur of the moment. He must have noticed the dog alone in the backyard and seen his opportunity. "Were you home today, Denise? Did you notice anyone out on the street?"

"I noticed lots of people. You looking for someone specific?"

"Probably a stranger to town. Perhaps an older man with a beard?"

"You think this guy took Alfred?" Gertie's sharp eyes darted from him to her backyard. "I knew he didn't escape on his own. I had the fence repaired before I adopted him."

"I didn't notice anyone like that," Denise said.

Zak blinked, absorbing the disappointment that yet another line of inquiry hadn't made it out of the starting gate.

Denise shifted her jaw to one side. Pondered. "But I remember the barking and crying stopping about halfway through the weather report. Could that have been when the pup was stolen?"

This sounded hopeful. "May have been. Do you recall the time?"

"Close to two thirty."

No description of the perp, but at least he had a time to work with. "If you remember anything more, any detail from today that stands out as strange, call the office right away."

He left the two women and went to canvass the neighbors across the street and on the other side of Gertie's house, as well as those whose yards backed onto Gertie's.

Most had been at jobs during the day. But the senior couple whose house backed Gertie's told a similar story to

Denise. They'd been relieved around two thirty when the dog stopped barking and crying but hadn't seen the cause for it. Two thirty, it seemed, was when they were usually down for their afternoon nap.

✕

AS A VOLUNTEER for the local search and rescue, Tiff had a day bag packed and ready to go at a moment's notice. So when she got the call from Kenny all she had to do was change into her black hiking pants and grab her yellow jacket.

As she prepared, she heard her mother take a call in the kitchen. A moment later Rosemary met her in the mudroom that led to the garage. Her mom was pulling her car keys out of her purse.

"I'm going to Justin's house to keep an eye on Geneva and Ashley so Justin and Debbie-Ann can join in the search."

Tiff nodded. That was good. They needed as many able-bodied searchers as possible. She opened the garage, then gave her mother a hug. "Try not to worry, Mom. I'll keep you posted how things are going."

"Poor Patsy and Chris. They'll be out of their minds with worry."

Tiff knew they wouldn't be the only ones. Her mother, having raised and lost a boy with a serious heart defect, knew what it was to face a parent's worst nightmare.

"We'll find her." Tiff had no basis to make the promise. Yet it came out anyway.

"I just pray that you do." Her mom kissed Tiff's forehead. "Be careful, honey. And don't worry about me. You have more urgent matters to tend to."

KENNY HAD SET up the command post in the picnic shelter at Lost Creek Park. Tiff lined up with the other volunteers and when it was her turn to check in, Kenny gave her shoulder a squeeze.

"Thanks for coming out. You've got a GPS unit and radio, so I'm putting you in charge of Sierra Four. Your group will search the forest to the east of the park."

"What are the other groups doing?"

"Sierra One is canvassing door to door in town, Sierra Two is headed up Strawberry Mountain, and Sierra Three is focusing on the bank of Lost Creek itself. With spring runoff, the water is high and the current fast. I sure hope Darby didn't go anywhere near there."

Tiff shuddered. She hoped so too.

Kenny assigned Justin and Debbie-Ann to her group, along with eight others. Tiff relayed the instructions she'd been given. "We'll move out in a line with about four feet between each of us. We're looking for Darby, obviously, but also evidence. This could be bits of clothing, or even a small piece of fabric snagged on a branch. We also have to watch for evidence of a small dog, a terrier mix named Alfred. If we find him, we'll want to avoid touching his collar or any rope that may be attached to it. Understood?"

Everyone nodded. Tiff glanced at her watch. They had about two and a half hours before sunset. "Let's make the most of the daylight."

There were murmurs of agreement as she led them beyond the park boundary to the edge of the forest. The eight of them formed a line, holding out their arms to assist in their spacing. Then they moved out.

The forest didn't make it easy on them and Tiff was glad she'd worn thick hiking pants, long socks and proper hiking boots. The trees themselves were typically several feet apart—they'd never get the sunlight they needed to survive otherwise—but the undergrowth was full of dry sticks that poked, thorns that scratched, and deadfall that required climbing over, or in some cases, under.

They had to navigate all of this, while keeping a keen eye for the smallest of clues that might help them find the little girl—or identify her abductor.

Kenny hadn't specified whether Darby was lost or had been kidnapped, but Tiff was almost positive it was the latter. She knew Patsy and her family well. Darby wasn't the kind of girl to go venturing out into the forest on her own. Like her mother, Darby was a people person. She loved chatting and socializing.

Besides, the town had been alerted to a man on the prowl, hanging around small children. If he had Darby, they had to find her quickly.

In formation with her team, Tiff marched through the forest. The undergrowth was full of optical illusions. What seemed to be a red piece of fabric was simply a colored barberry leaf. What looked like a child's shoe turned into an oddly shaped piece of rotting wood.

To her left, Justin was focused on the search as intently as if his own daughter was missing. His jaw was set, his hands clenched. On his other side was Debbie-Ann. Earlier, Tiff had seen tears in her eyes. She guessed this must be especially difficult for those who had children. They must be thinking, *there but for the grace of God...*

"Have you heard anything more from Clark?" she asked her brother, keeping her eyes on the terrain.

"No. I drove by his place on my way here. His car was missing. I'm not sure where he would have gone."

"I guess it's too much to hope he's left town already?"

"If only it could be that easy. It would be a hell of a relief."

"For Mom and me, too. Especially Mom. Thanks for taking that stand and giving Clark an ultimatum."

"I wish I'd stood up to Clark earlier. I really thought he had my best interests at heart. I was a damned fool."

"It's in our nature to trust our family, or the people we believe are family. Mom and I trusted Marsha, remember."

Tiff sensed a movement on the ground, close to her. She stopped and looked at a pile of dead leaves trapped against the trunk of a fallen, rotting ponderosa pine tree. As she stared, the leaves rustled again. Was it the wind? Then Tiff heard a quiet whimper.

"Hold it." She put her hand up. A little brown nose poked out of the leaves. She crouched and brushed away some of the leaves. Sad brown eyes gazed up at her from a mostly black face. The rest of the dog's body was white with a few black spots. He looked like he weighed about twenty-five pounds.

"I think I've found our dog." Tiff allowed a spark of hope. Maybe this meant Darby was near? As she brushed aside more of the leaves, the dog nuzzled her hand. Poor thing must be scared.

Remembering the instructions to avoid touching the collar, she managed a look at the tags. "Yup. His name is Alfred. And there's a bit of yellow rope tied to his collar." She reached for her radio.

"Sierra Four to command post. Come in."

"Command post." Kenny's voice came through clearly. "Sierra Four go ahead."

"We've found the dog. He's got a tag on his collar that says 'Alfred.'"

"Great. Any sign of Darby?"

"Not yet."

"Okay. Can you send someone back with the dog while

the rest of the team keeps searching?"

Justin stepped forward. "I'll take the dog back and then rejoin the group."

Tiff glanced behind her. They'd traveled about three hundred yards from the park boundary. She had no doubt Justin could easily navigate to the command post and back.

"You'll have to carry him. He's awfully tired and weak." She wrinkled her nose. "He doesn't smell that great either. Looks like he's had diarrhea."

"Poor guy." Justin gathered the dog in his arms. "I won't be long," he said, looking at Debbie-Ann. She gave him an encouraging nod and a smile.

"Right then." Tiff surveyed her group. The find appeared to have reenergized them. "Let's keep moving, folks. If Darby was following this puppy she could be nearby."

Chapter Twenty

"HERE'S HOW I think it happened." Zak and Nadine were in his office. They'd finished collecting evidence from the Larkin house and left Bea to sit with Patsy and Bonnie for a few hours. Until the FBI arrived, Zak wanted to keep the crime scene pristine.

"Go on." Nadine crunched into an apple from the bowl on his desk.

Zak grabbed one too.

"The perp may have cased out Darby's room earlier and seen the posters of cute puppies on the wall. Or maybe he just assumed all kids like dogs. In either case, when he noticed Alfred alone in Gertie Humphrey's yard, he nabbed him. Based on the time Gertie's neighbors noticed the dog stop barking this would have been around two thirty in the afternoon."

"With you so far."

"The next thing our perp does is tie the dog to a tree directly across from the gate that divides the Larkins' yard from the forest. Then he pries open Darby's window, so she'll hear the puppy cry when she gets home from school."

"How did he make it cry? I hope he didn't hurt him." Nadine sounded appalled, as if hurting a puppy would be a line a man kidnapping a child wouldn't cross.

"Tiff found the dog unharmed, remember? Anyway, the perp didn't need to hurt Alfred. He could have found a recording of a crying puppy on the internet and played that."

"Right. I should have thought of that."

Nadine discreetly rubbed a tear from her eye. Zak regarded her closely. It wasn't like her to be so emotional. It had to be stress. He knew his entire staff was exhausted to a point where they could miss something. Make a mistake. They'd given their all trying to find Sybil. And now to have a second missing person. A *child*.

"What time did Darby get home from school?" Nadine asked.

"Around quarter to four. She spent a little time in the kitchen with her mother having a snack. It was probably at least fifteen or twenty minutes later that she went to her bedroom."

"The perp would have been hiding in the forest, watching her window…"

"Yes," Zak agreed. "Earlier he must have opened the gate, so Darby could see Alfred in the forest, just beyond her yard. Darby knows her mother is against having a dog as a pet. But if she rescues this dog, and if her mom sees he has no other home. Well, her mom will have to give in then."

"That sounds like the way a kid would think. It's how I

thought at her age," Nadine allowed. "So Darby puts on her shoes at the back door."

"Which isn't visible from the kitchen, where her mother was working on admin stuff for the café," Zak added. It was an important detail.

"Right. She puts on her shoes—unseen by her mother—and quietly slips into the yard. When she reaches the puppy..."

"The perp comes out of hiding and nabs her. He must have surprised her from behind and covered her mouth, to muffle any screaming." Poor kid would have been so terrified. Especially when she recognized him as the man who'd been watching her.

"And then what?" Nadine asked.

"He had to get Darby to his truck, but first he cut the dog loose."

"Gosh. How nice of him." Nadine tossed her apple core across the room. It fell in a perfect arc, landing with a thud in the trash can meant for recycling.

Zak went to the topo map hanging next to his whiteboard. "The trail that runs behind the Larkin place also goes by Sybil's road and ends up here, at Lost Creek Park. I figure he'd left his truck in that corner of the lot."

"So, this clinches it, then?" Nadine asked. "Darby isn't simply missing. She's been kidnapped."

Zak wanted to believe it was still possible Darby was at a friend's place. Or innocently lost in the forest. But the evidence said otherwise. The scrape marks on the outside of Darby's window. The piece of yellow cord beyond the gate. And Alfred, with the other end of the yellow cord tied to his collar.

"She's been kidnapped," Zak said.

IT WAS PAST eleven when Zak left Nadine at the office, manning their phone, email and social media platforms in case any information came in as a result of the Amber Alert. He was going to the Larkin residence to relieve Bea so she could grab a few hours of sleep.

Patsy and Chris weren't on Zak's suspect radar, but in a typical child abduction case, parents were often prime suspects. Zak was curious to see how the FBI would proceed when they got here. Some sheriffs hated when state or national law enforcers came onto their turf. Zak didn't feel that way. He welcomed the help. Sybil and Darby's safety were what mattered here, not his ego.

As Zak drove down the streets of his town, silence pressed in on him. Not peaceful, but sinister. Something evil was at work in this town. He wanted to fight it, but every time he tried to land a punch, all he hit was air.

An hour earlier Sierra One had reported in. They'd knocked on every door in this town. They'd had pictures of Darby and a description of a man with a beard driving a dark-colored pickup truck. But the search had come up blank, not a single lead.

Sierra Two, Three and Four were still working, using headlamps and flashlights to penetrate the new enemy—night. The wind had kicked up in the past four hours and shifted to the north. According to National Weather Service an unexpected cold front was blowing in, along with a pile of moisture. In other words, Zak could expect snow to start falling sometime after midnight.

Unexpected storms happened in May all the time. But did it have to come now?

Zak pushed on, his legs heavier with each step…as if the calcium in his bones had been replaced with lead. He and his team were being asked to run a marathon when they'd only trained for a sprint.

The Larkins' was the only house on the block with the lights still on, both inside and out. When Zak knocked, Bea opened the door. Despite dark circles under her eyes and a weary set to her shoulders, she moved briskly to usher him inside.

"Any news?"

"Sorry no," he said loud enough so that Patsy and Bonnie, who'd come to the door off the kitchen, could hear.

The women returned to the kitchen table and he followed them there. A game of double solitaire was laid out on the table, along with a plate of sandwiches, a bottle of brandy and three glasses.

"I'm sorry, Patsy. Bonnie. I wish I had some encouraging news."

"Waiting is the worst." Elbows on the table, Patsy bowed her head and dug her fingers through her hair.

"Try to eat one of these sandwiches, love." Bonnie reached out to her daughter, eyes glazed with tears. "You need to keep up your strength."

Patsy inhaled a breath that sounded more like a shudder. She raised her head slightly. "I appreciate you trying to distract me with that card game, Bea, and it was nice of the neighbors to bring over sandwiches, but I should be out there. Looking for her. It's dark now. She'll be so scared…"

"Half the town is out looking for your daughter," Zak said. "But this is Darby's home and you're her mom. You need to be here."

Patsy looked like she'd aged ten years since he'd seen her last. He noticed her phone on the counter, plugged in to a power source.

"What if Darby finds her way home and you aren't here?" Zak turned to Bea. "Go home and get some rest. I'll stay for a while." He'd set up in the dining room where he could keep in touch with Kenny and the state police while completing his paperwork. He wanted everything completed, every "i" dotted and "t" crossed before the FBI showed up.

⨯

NADINE TRIED TO focus on her reports, but her eyes were continually pulled to the window next to her desk. At this time of night, her only reward was her reflection. Yet she couldn't seem to stop herself from checking.

She got up from her desk. Stretched out her back. Her shoulders. Then touched her toes.

Once more she was drawn to the window. She pressed her nose to the glass, cupping her hands on either side of her eyes. Outside it was snowing. Big, fat flakes flying at a forty-five-degree angle. The unexpected spring storm was here.

She hoped Darby and Sybil were somewhere warm and dry.

And together?

She and Zak hadn't discussed the possibility that the same man had abducted both of them, but despite the lack of evidence, she knew he was thinking it. How could he not? In a county with less than three thousand people, how could there be two kidnappers at work?

The piles of reports and files on her desk mocked her. She, Zak, Kenny and Bea had worked so hard these past five days, yet it seemed they were no closer to finding out what was going on. It wasn't fair. They'd followed up on every possible lead. They'd been meticulous about collecting evidence. They'd interviewed almost everyone in town.

Yet where did it all lead?

Nadine wondered if word of Darby's disappearance had made it out to the Woodrows. Maybe Amber and her dad heard the bulletin over the radio while they were eating dinner. Or saw it on the local news later, while watching TV. It made her sad to picture the two of them, together, yet alone in their unhappiness. She wondered how often Pete Woodrow hit the bottle. What did Amber do then—cower in her bedroom?

It wasn't fair what some kids had to go through. Zak didn't talk about his childhood often, but Nadine knew he'd been bullied by his father and older brothers, both verbally and physically. Some kids might have been broken by what he'd gone through, instead Zak had developed a quiet, inner strength.

Nadine, in contrast, had been lucky. Her parents were wonderful. They'd encouraged her love of riding, driving her to the stables and footing the expensive bills for lessons and equipment. She'd had to plead for permission to attend her first rodeo clinic, but once they'd finally given in, and seen how much she loved the sport, they'd been her champions there, too.

More than that, they'd created a home that was both safe and fun. A place with rules but also laughter. And everything they'd done for her and her interests, they'd also done for her brother Dylan and his obsession with hockey.

If only all children could have what she'd had. After seeing Darby's home, her room, and what she knew of her parents, Nadine figured Darby was one of the lucky ones. At least she had been.

Ringing from the main phone cut into her thoughts. Nadine grabbed the receiver. "Lost Trail Sheriff Department."

"I-Is that Deputy Black?"

The young woman speaking sounded worried, yet tentative. And though Nadine had never spoken to her on the phone before, she recognized her voice.

"Yes, this is Deputy Black. Am I speaking to Amber Woodrow?"

"Yeah."

Nadine jumped into the pause that followed. "Are you okay, Amber?"

"I'm good. I'm not calling about myself. It's my father…"

This time Nadine gave the young woman time to collect herself. Finally, she continued.

"I'm worried about my dad. He told me he'd be home for supper."

It was past midnight now. "Does he have a cell phone with him?"

"Yeah. I've tried calling him, but he isn't answering. His phone could be out of power. He always forgets to charge it."

"What was he doing this afternoon?"

"He was cultivating the west quarter. I was worried he might have had an accident with the cultivator so around seven I rode my bike out to the field to check on him. The tractor and cultivator were fine, but his truck was missing."

So, he'd gone somewhere. Hopefully not too far, in this weather.

One of the consequences of living between two mountain ranges was unpredictable weather. And spring blizzards could be the worst. The warmer spring air usually produced fat, moisture-rich snowflakes that were blinding as they fell and accumulated quickly.

"Do you have any idea where he could have gone?"

"I've already phoned all our neighbors. No one's seen him. I don't know what to do. If it wasn't snowing, I'd go out looking for him on my bike."

"No, no, you don't want to do that." She gave the matter some thought. "Tell you what, I'll take a quick drive around town and see if I can spot his truck. Maybe he went to the Dew Drop and forgot to tell you."

She heard the sigh of relief on the other end. "Yes. He does go there sometimes."

"I'll call you right back."

Nadine phoned the pub, but no one answered. Must be too busy. She'd have to dash over and check for herself. As soon as she stepped outside, she was blasted by the cold wind and icy snow. Scrunching the lapels of her coat close to her neck, Nadine ran for her truck.

There were no vehicles parked outside the Bavarian-styled pub and a note was taped on the locked front door. *Sorry, we're closed. Mari and I have been called out by search and rescue.* It was signed by Keith Dewy, the proprietor.

Well, hell.

Nadine ran back to her truck and drove the main streets of the town. But there was no sign of Pete Woodrow, or his truck.

Chapter Twenty-One

May 8

KNOWING THE COMING snow might hide crucial evidence, search and rescue worked hard into the night. By two in the morning, the town and surrounding areas had been combed thoroughly. With six inches of snow already on the ground, and no let-up in the deluge, Zak called Kenny and gave permission to halt the search.

"Get some rest and we'll see what the morning brings."

"Okay, Zak. I'm sorry we didn't find her."

Kenny sounded exhausted. Dispirited.

"Tomorrow's another day. We won't give up."

Ten minutes later, Chris and Trevor Larkin arrived home. Trevor hugged his mother and grandmother then went to collapse in his bed. Chris grabbed a shower then poured himself a glass of brandy and joined his wife and mother-in-law in the family room.

Patsy and her mother were curled up on either side of the sofa. Zak had started a fire in the wood-burning stove, hoping it would provide a bit of warmth and comfort.

At one point Zak let his head drop to the dining room

table and nodded off for a bit. When he awoke, thirty minutes later, he went to check on the Larkins. They were all sleeping too, Patsy and Bonnie on the sofa and Chris sprawled out in a reclining chair. At some point Trevor had come out of his room and joined them. He was on the floor near the fire, with a pillow and a fluffy quilt.

Quietly Zak added more wood pellets to the fire. With the lights in the house on dim, he could see out the patio doors that led to the yard. About ten inches of snow were piled on the patio furniture. And still the snow was coming.

THE FAMILY AWOKE an hour before dawn. They moved like zombies through a semblance of morning routine. Chris put on a pot of coffee and Patsy sliced cinnamon buns in half, then toasted and buttered them. Zak accepted the breakfast. Though he didn't have much appetite, the family had even less.

At seven o'clock Bea came to spell him off. Zak went to the front door to let her in.

Bea had clearly showered and changed her top, but her face was as haggard as the night before.

"I slept at my sister's here in town. Didn't want to deal with country roads in this storm."

Eighteen inches of snow, as pristine as wedding cake frosting, was now stacked on Zak's truck.

"Good thinking," Zak said quietly, not wanting to disturb the family in the other room. "I've heard from the FBI. They're not sure when they can get here. The Missoula airport is closed due to weather. Plus, the state police have closed the highway at the pass."

Bea shrugged. As happened from time to time, Lost Trail was on its own. They had all learned to accept it when it happened.

Leaving Bea with the Larkins, Zak went home to shower and change and feed his cat. It was quarter to eight when he arrived at the office. He found Nadine asleep on the cot in the holding cell, her phone and radio next to her on the pillow. He wanted to let her rest, but she had a dog and a horse at home who needed food and water, and in Junior's case, a chance to get outside and relieve himself.

He placed his hand on her check. "Hey, babe."

She moaned and turned in to his touch. Then her eyes flew open. "Zak."

"Hate to wake you but it's almost eight."

"Chores," she murmured. Her gaze moved beyond Zak to the bars of the lockup. Suddenly she sat up tall. "Have we found her?"

Zak shook his head and she let out a long, tired sigh. "Of course not. You would have said something. Sorry, Zak. My brain feels a little scrambled this morning."

They went through the short hallway to the main office. As Nadine was putting on her jacket, she told him about the call she'd received from Amber Woodrow last night.

"Once I'm done with my chores, I'd like to drive out that way and see if I can find Pete."

Zak considered the idea. "Go ahead. The state police have closed the pass, but the roads aren't too bad here in the valley. Plus, you can keep an eye out for any suspicious activity. Search and rescue didn't find anything close to town. If Darby and Sybil are still in our county, that leaves a lot of ground for us to cover."

"Will do." Nadine was about to leave, then changed tack and gave him a kiss. A very nice kiss. When it was over, she pulled back and looked at him. "You're doing a good job, Zak. It may not feel that way. But you are."

And then she left.

As he put on the coffee, he thought fondly of his days as dispatcher, when this had been his regular responsibility and the weight of running the entire office hadn't yet been his burden.

Though Sheriff Ford had had his weaknesses, Zak now understood he'd underestimated the pressure on the guy. Once the FBI got here, they'd be pushing to control the case. And he would end up acquiescing. He had to. One sheriff, two deputies and a dispatcher just could not handle this situation anymore.

It hurt to admit, but there it was. His first unsolved case.

Thirty minutes later, when Kenny showed up looking better than a man who had grabbed five hours sleep at best ought to look, Zak was on his second coffee. He waited for Kenny to hang up his jacket and fill his own mug, before inviting him into his office to study the topo map.

"I want to cover as much of the county as possible before the Feds come." He showed Kenny the route Nadine was planning to patrol to the south. "I was thinking you should drive out north to the ski hill today. Season's been over for a month now. Check out the lodge, the condo complexes and private chalets. So many vacant buildings add up to a lot of possible hiding places."

Zak sank into his chair once Kenny had left. Finally, he had a moment of quiet, to sit and reflect. His intuition told him random patrols were not going to find Darby and Sybil. Checking fingerprints, tire treads, search and rescue…all of these standard procedures had been necessary…but they weren't going to find Darby and Sybil either.

What he needed was to start at the beginning. Sybil's disappearance. No evidence linked what had happened to her with Darby's disappearance, other than a vague description of an older man with a beard.

But he felt they had to be connected. He'd lived in Lost Trail all his life. He knew the people here, their problems, their feuds, this issue. This was different.

Zak paced his office, wishing he had time to go for a run. The exercise would clear his brain, help him see what he was missing.

Instead, he put on a fresh pot of coffee and ate one of

Nadine's apples.

Sybil. Everyone in town loved her. No one could imagine anyone wanting to hurt her. Yet it was possible someone had.

Why?

From the beginning he'd focused on the men Sybil had met on the dating site, assuming one of them had written the anonymous letter that Sybil received the very day she disappeared. The letter had worried Sybil enough that she'd made a note to tell him about it. Only she hadn't had the chance.

What if the dating site had been a distraction?

I want a second chance. You owe me.

Was it a coincidence Sybil had received that letter just a few days before May the 5th, the date that had little black hearts beside it in her Day-Timer? She was always a little sad in the spring, Sybil had told her friends. Yet none of them knew why.

Despite her friendly personality, it turned out that Sybil was a very private person.

He'd run this case assuming she was a woman with nothing to hide.

What if he was wrong about that?

Zak grabbed his jacket and gave Bea a call. She would have to leave the Larkins and come back to the office to man the phones. In the meantime, he would be at Sybil Tombe's house.

The snow had stopped, but the wind was still fierce. The town looked like it was the dead of winter. He drove north on Sybil's street until the road dead-ended. None of Sybil's neighbors had shoveled their driveways yet. Maybe they were planning to wait for the melt. This was May. It wouldn't take long.

Zak waded through the snow toward Sybil's front door. Inside, his gaze swept over the now familiar rooms. They'd gone through this house so many times. He was probably foolish to think there was something they might have missed.

But this time he was going to imagine he was a woman with a secret. Something important, something none of her friends knew about. Something that made her sad every year at the beginning of May.

Zak dismissed the main living areas. Briefly he considered the office, before moving instead to the bedroom. They'd already looked through Sybil's nightstand and medicine cabinets, her closet and dresser and the chest at the foot of her bed.

He would look again.

The nightstand and medicine cabinets were easy. He remembered every item from the first time he'd looked. Next was the dresser. He checked under the piles of undergarments and T-shirts and sweaters, feeling carefully for something that might be hidden between the folds of fabric. Nothing.

Then he went to her closet. He searched the shelf at the

top and the boxes piled at the bottom. He found old yearbooks and photo albums from her childhood. First time he'd seen these, he'd paged through in a rush. Today he went slowly. Methodically. The stories he found here matched those he'd been told by Sybil's friends. No secrets. No leads.

He repacked the boxes and pushed them to the back in the closet.

One last place to check…the trunk at the foot of Sybil's bed. It was cedar lined and full of handmade quilts. Maybe her mother had made them. Or grandmother. They were very soft and faded.

He decided to pull them out, and unfold them. There were four quilts in the trunk, all with beautiful patterns, and carrying the woodsy scent of cedar. By the time he reached the last of the quilts, he'd concluded he was wasting his time.

But then something heavy dropped out from the folds of the quilt.

It was a photo album.

Right away Zak could tell this one was different from the others in the closet.

There was a stylized picture of a baby on the cover, along with the embossed words, "Baby's First Year."

Zak took the book to the kitchen where the lighting was better.

AS SHE DROVE her truck south, studded tires plowing fresh tracks through the accumulated snow, Nadine had the uncanny sensation of moving backward. Partly it was the disorienting effect of the all-white landscape. But mostly her mental landscape was the problem. She felt as if her brain was stalled, grinding repetitively through the same thought patterns, never making any progress.

The fatigue didn't help. She'd never felt anything like it before. Not even in her rodeo days when she'd sometimes had to drive over twelve hours a day, and then compete that night.

She'd dated her share of cowboys back then. Some of them gorgeous, some of them charming, all of them wild and fun. With Zak she'd found something different. He was solid and smart. Dependable without being boring. There wasn't one cowboy she would have considered spending the rest of her life with. Whereas Zak…

Yes, Zak was different. But they'd never really discussed the future. She had no idea if he was interested in marriage or a family. Or even moving in together.

She tapped her steering wheel to a beat going on in her head. "*Big wheels keep on turning—*" And hers were. They just weren't getting anywhere.

So many missing people: Sybil, Gray-Beard, Darby. Now Pete Woodrow too. And so much wilderness to hide or get lost in. If a person wanted to live under the radar, they could hardly pick a better spot than Lost Trail, Montana. This county was perfect for hiding dirty secrets, even if one of those secrets was a body.

Nadine made it all the way to Boundary Road without passing another vehicle. As she approached the Woodrows' house, she slowed, preparing to turn in. She didn't see Pete's truck parked anywhere on the property. But she ought to check in with Amber anyway. Maybe her father had found a way to leave her a message that he was okay.

Amber came to the door in baggy gray sweatpants, an oversized T-shirt and a novel in her hand. "Have you—?"

Nadine shook her head before Amber finished the question. "I take it you haven't heard from him either?"

"No. I'm trying to distract myself with a story, but I keep reading the same paragraph over and over."

"Okay. Well, I'll check up the road a ways. You're sure he isn't visiting one of the neighbors?"

"Last night I called everyone I could think of."

Nadine went to leave. "Keep your phone on. I'll let you know as soon as I find something."

Amber followed her to the door, looking like a child who wanted to be told everything would be okay. But Amber, more than most young women her age, knew there were no such guarantees in life.

Back in her truck, Nadine continued down the road, wondering if she ought to report in with Zak. All he needed was to be told yet another citizen of their county had gone missing.

Just as she was reaching for the radio, she noticed a spot of dark gray in the distance. As she closed the distance, the splotch of color took shape. It was a pickup truck.

Looked like it had veered off the road to the right, into the snow-filled ditch.

She kept driving until she could see inside the driver's side window.

It was Pete Woodrow all right. He was slumped against the headrest with his mouth hanging open.

ON THE FIRST page of the album a baby name was written: Jessica Jean Graves. The mother was listed as Sybil Tombe. The father, Russell Graves.

Zak did a double take. Why had no one told him that Sybil had a baby?

More data followed. The birth date was September 20th, 1979. The baby had weighed six pounds and five ounces at birth. Her length was twenty inches.

On the next page were three photographs. First, a red, wrinkly, tiny baby with eyes scrunched closed, mouth pursed in a bow. In the next photo the baby was wrapped in a pink blanket and being held by a proud young mother. The mother was very thin, with a mop of curly hair and a sweet smile. A much younger Sybil.

The final photo on the page was of a young man holding

the baby, presumably the father. He had a long, lean face, brown hair and a slight build. He looked pleased, but also a bit dazed.

The next page was meant to record people who had visited in the hospital and gifts that had been received. Nothing had been written here.

Zak moved on to a page where proud parents were to record developmental milestones. The first couple of items had been filled in with what Zak now recognized to be Sybil's writing.

My first smile…*two months*, Sybil had written.

My first tooth…*four months.*

I first rolled over…

I first sat up by myself…

I started to crawl…

My first step…

Sybil must have lost interest in the book, because none of the later milestones were filled in.

The rest of the book was filled with photographs. Some of them were taken outside, in what seemed to be a big city. The baby quickly gained weight and developed cute pudgy cheeks. A picture of her asleep in her crib drew Zak's attention. There, in the bed with her, was the teddy bear he'd found in Sybil's kitchen.

Zak's throat went dry. He wanted to put the book down and not look any further. Sybil must have had her reasons for keeping her baby's existence a secret. By handling this book and looking through it he was invading her most precious and private possession.

But he had to keep looking. This could be the key to everything.

He turned another page. The baby was growing. Her bald head developed silky, fair hair. She had a beautiful smile. A real cutie. But as he progressed through the photographs Zak began to notice something strange.

In every photo baby Jessica was either being held or laying in her crib or on a blanket.

There were no pictures of her sitting up, crawling, or walking. No reaching for toys. Not even holding her head erect.

Also…Sybil and the baby's father's expressions were changing too. Proud smiles were replaced with anxious, strained ones.

Toward the end of the book was a photo of a birthday cake with a single candle. Another photo had Sybil holding Jessica in her arms, while giving the child a taste of the icing. The baby, though smiling with delight, was as limp as if she were asleep.

There were a few more photos after the birthday. But then nothing. The final five pages of the book were completely blank.

Zak closed the book. This was important information and he needed to go back to the office and get to work. But his body felt too heavy to lift from the chair. A great sadness pressed in on him.

He had a good idea why there were no more photos in the book. Why Sybil never spoke of her child. Jessica must have died a short time after her first birthday.

He wasn't a parent, but he could imagine the pain this must have caused Sybil. He thought of the little teddy bear with the spots worn off from being "loved" too much. Jessica hadn't been capable of playing with her toys. So, it must have been Sybil who had held the little bear…and cried more than a few tears into its fur.

Chapter Twenty-Two

"PETE! PETE! WAKE up!" Nadine shook the man's shoulders. She might have worried he'd had a heart attack, except for the stench of alcohol and the empty fifth of rye on the passenger seat.

"Huh?" Pete opened his eyes, then closed them quickly. "God, it's bright out."

"Yeah, we had a little snow last night." She stepped back from the open driver's side door and put a hand on her hip. What a mess this man was.

Pete tried opening his eyes again, this time just a fraction. "You're the deputy who came by the house the other day."

"That's right. Deputy Black. Your daughter phoned me last night. She was worried when you didn't come home."

"Aw shit. I should phone her…" He reached for the cell phone in his cupholder. "Damn. I'm out of power." He turned the key in his ignition and when nothing happened, swore. "Looks like I'm out of gas, too."

"I'll call her," Nadine offered. Pete needed to collect himself a little before he spoke to Amber. "See if you can make your way out of this ditch and I'll give you a ride home."

"But my truck…"

"You're going to need a tow to get your truck out of this mess." Nadine waded through the knee-high snow, climbing up the side of the ditch until she was back on level ground. She'd put on her emergency lights in case another vehicle happened along, but that hadn't happened. No matter which direction she turned, there was only snow and land and trees and sky.

She rang Amber's number.

"Your dad's okay. His truck went off the road and got stuck in some snow. I'll give him a ride home. Shouldn't be long."

"Oh, Deputy Black, thank you so much!"

Nadine didn't think Pete was much of a father. She wondered if he had any idea how lucky he was to have a caring daughter like Amber.

Meanwhile Pete was making slow progress out of the ditch. Two times he fell into the snow and had to pull himself out of it. Nadine didn't offer to help. The exercise was good for him. And the cold would help clear his mind.

When he finally made it to her truck, she handed him her water bottle.

"You should drink this."

He downed every drop and looked like he needed more.

Nadine leaned against her truck and crossed her arms.

"So. You want to tell me what happened?"

Pete took a wide-legged stance and shoved his hands into his jacket pockets. He cleared his throat, and she thought he was going to speak, but he didn't.

Nadine shifted her weight from one leg to the other. Then she tilted her head and raised her sunglasses. "Well?"

With his gaze fixed on the field beyond his truck, Pete finally began. "Iris was the heart and soul of our family. It's my fault she's gone. I wish I could take her place, but since I can't, I'm just doing my best to keep this farm running. I'm doing it partly for Amber, so she'll have a home, and partly because I don't know what else to do with myself."

Nadine had seen expressions like Pete's on the nightly news, on men in disaster zones who had lost their families and homes. She felt suddenly humbled. In the face of what he had suffered, how dared she judge?

"Sometimes it gets to me and I just want to black it all out. I tell Amber I'm going to the Dew Drop in town, because that sounds at least somewhat socially acceptable."

"But you don't go there."

"Nah. I get a bottle and drive myself to the middle of nowhere and get plastered. I drink until I can't remember why I'm drinking. And then I sleep. And when I wake up, I drive home. Usually I manage to get home while Amber's still in bed."

He stopped talking and Nadine let the silence settle between them for a few moments.

He finally looked her straight on. “Believe it or not, I enjoy the hangover. I like feeling bad. It’s what I deserve.”

Nadine shook her head. “You need to talk to someone. A counselor or something.”

“I talk to Iris. That’s good enough for me.” He cleared his throat again. “Should we get moving?”

“Right.” She patted the side of her truck. “Get in and I’ll drive you home.”

After Amber’s call last night, she’d wondered if Pete could be the one who had kidnapped Sybil and Darby. Obviously, this was not the case. He was just a man broken by guilt and grief.

There were more people like that in this world than Nadine had ever suspected.

WIND BLASTED ZAK’S truck as he plowed his way back to the office. On the way, he phoned Rosemary Masterson. “Do you know if Sybil ever got married, or had a baby?”

“What?” Rosemary sounded incredulous. “Why would you ask such a thing? Obviously I would have told you if she had.”

“Did she ever mention Russell Graves to you? Or someone named Jessica?”

“N—”

“Don’t answer right away. I want you to really think

about it."

A few seconds went by. Then Rosemary spoke, her tone calmer and softer. "Zak, I assure you I've never heard Sybil speak about either of those people. We may have drifted apart for a few years when she was doing her postdoc in Boston, but if she'd gotten married, or had a baby, she would have told me. I'm sure of it."

"Okay."

"Zak, who are those people? Why were you asking about them?"

"I can't go into it right now."

He didn't want to bust Sybil's secret. He'd just needed to confirm that Sybil's oldest friend in town had no idea about Russell or the baby.

Bea was at her desk when he pushed through the main door.

She held up a yellow sticky note. "Special Agent Bridge from the FBI just called. She's flying into Missoula tomorrow and renting a car. She should be here around two in the afternoon."

"Good to know." He took the note with Special Agent Bridge's name and contact information, even though he couldn't be less interested. He finally had a lead that felt like something. "I have something to show you. Can you come to my office a minute?"

"Only if you take the time to eat one of the oatmeal apple muffins Harvey baked. I put them next to the coffee machine."

Zak didn't feel hungry, but this was going to be a long day, so he wheeled around and grabbed two of the muffins. Bea's husband liked to bake, and she often brought cookies or muffins to work.

In his office, he carefully slipped the photo album out of the plastic bag he'd used to carry it out of Sybil's house. "I found this at the bottom of a trunk with some old quilts." He placed the album on the table and gestured for Bea to sit down and take a look.

While she slowly examined each page, he wolfed down the muffins then went to grab a coffee. By the time he'd returned, Bea was closing the book.

"Oh my, Zak. That is unbelievable. Sybil had a baby. And a husband."

"You knew nothing about them?"

"No." Bea's large hoop earrings swayed as she shook her head. "I can't imagine why Sybil kept them a secret for all these years. I wonder what happened to that poor baby. And her husband. What was his name again?"

"Russell Graves," Zak said. "I don't think he and Sybil were married. I've looked at all the pictures carefully and neither of them wore a ring."

"I didn't pick up on that." Bea looked impressed. "I guess they just lived together."

"The only years Sybil lived outside of Montana were the three she spent getting her postdoc in Boston. Looking at the background of some of those photos, I'd guess that's where these were taken."

"Must be. But, Zak. You don't think this has anything to do with Sybil's disappearance? This all happened forty years ago. Ancient history, as they say. Look at these photos of Sybil. She's practically a kid."

Bea had a point. Forty years was a long time. But this had been a defining point in Sybil's life. Zak believed it had to be relevant.

"Yeah, it was a long time ago. I'd still like you to make a copy of this book for our records."

"If you say so." Bea took the album and left.

Zak got on his computer. Social security numbers would make his job so much easier, if only he had them. He'd bet there were a lot of men named Russell Graves in the United States between the ages of, say, fifty-five to sixty-five.

But there wouldn't be so many Jessica Jean Graves who had been born in Boston in 1979 and died a year or two later. Assuming, of course, that was what had happened. But it must be, or why were there no more photos? He'd start there.

A call to the relevant federal government department soon proved him right. He gave them all the information he had plus his Originating Agency ID Number, and in exchange they agreed to email a copy of the death certificate.

Soon Zak had a printed copy in his hands.

Jessica Jean Graves had died on May the fifth in 1980, at

one year of age. Her parents were listed as Sybil Tombe and Russell Graves. The residence provided was a Boston address.

Primary cause of death was smoke inhalation.

Manner of death was homicide.

Chapter Twenty-Three

When Nadine reached the top of the lane to Pete Woodrow's house, he had the passenger door open before she brought the truck to a complete stop.

"Thanks for the lift."

Nadine shook her head. He wasn't getting rid of her that easily. She turned off the ignition and pocketed her keys.

His forehead crinkled in a combination of pain and frown. "You need something?"

"I want to check in with Amber. She's the one who contacted our office, after all." Zak thought she should accept Gertie's assertion that Amber was fine, just dealing with the grief of losing her mother. But after this morning, Nadine wasn't buying it.

Pete's back was stiff with annoyance as she followed him toward the house, but at least this time he wasn't ordering her off his property.

Amber was waiting at the back door, her expression a mixture of relief and a fearful uncertainty that triggered alarm bells for Nadine.

"You okay, Dad?"

Pete hung his head as he passed by his daughter. "Yeah. Sorry I worried you. I'm going up to take a shower."

Amber chewed the inside of her cheek as she watched him pass through the kitchen then down the hallway.

Once he was out of sight, she expelled a heavy sigh. "Thank you so much for bringing him home. Where did you find him?"

"Down the road to the west, about ten miles." Nadine hesitated, not sure if she should tell Amber she thought her father needed counseling.

"You said the truck was in the ditch?"

Nadine nodded.

"We'll have to take the tractor and pull it out." Amber was pulling on her shirtsleeves again. Was it a habit? Or were there fresh bruises she was hiding?

"I should get back to work. But before I go, I want to make sure you're okay. Amber, I know you and your father are still grieving the loss of your mother. But I can't help feeling something else is troubling you."

She tried to look the young woman in her eyes, but Amber lowered her head, as if she was studying something on the floor. A few moments later, her shoulders started shaking.

Instinctively Nadine moved toward the young woman, reached out and gave her shoulders a gentle squeeze.

"What's wrong?" she asked quietly. "Is it your father? Are you afraid of him?"

Amber shook her head violently. Then pressed the heels of her hands to her eyes. "I'm sorry. I shouldn't have broken down like that. Lately I feel so emotional and so tired…it's like I'm not even myself anymore."

Emotional and tired.

Now didn't that sound familiar. Nadine took a closer look at Amber, trying to see past the baggy outfit, to the figure beneath. She wondered why she hadn't suspected sooner. "Are you pregnant, Amber?"

The young woman lifted her head. Her eyes sparkled with tears and her cheeks were flushed, but there was a determined set to her jaw.

"Yes," she admitted. "I think I'm close to six months."

Nadine felt a little light-headed. She sat in one of the kitchen chairs. She'd guessed as much, but hearing the news confirmed was still emotional.

"Do you want to talk about it?"

Amber pressed her lips together, then nodded. She sat in the chair at right angles to Nadine. "Last November some kids I knew from school talked me into going to a party out in the country. The parents were away and there was going to be a keg of beer. I told my father I was at a girlfriend's house for a sleepover. And I went."

Nadine had gone through similar escapades in her teenaged years. She nodded and waited for Amber to continue.

"A guy I liked was there. He's a year older than me. We got talking, and he seemed really into me. I didn't have any beer, but my girlfriend had made Jell-O shots and I tried them. They were actually pretty tasty, so I had a few." Amber shrugged. "I'm not trying to say I was so drunk I didn't know what I was doing. I was maybe a little drunk. But I did know what I was doing."

"So, you had sex with the guy?"

"He asked did I want to go upstairs, and I said I did. I thought he really liked me. But he never even text messaged me after that night." Amber's bottom lip trembled. "I only got the nerve to tell him I was pregnant ten days ago."

A floorboard squeaked behind them. Nadine turned at the same moment as Amber. Pete Woodrow was at the entrance to the kitchen, eyes wide, mouth gaping.

Instinctively Nadine put herself between Amber and her father. Pete's face was red and getting redder, his hands clenched like mallets at his sides. She was about to warn him to stay calm, when she saw his eyes. They were full of tears.

The big, muscular man seemed to get smaller and softer. He swiped his eyes with the back of his hand. "I noticed something was different about you. You should have told me."

"Sorry, Dad," Amber said softly.

In a flash Nadine could see she'd worried for nothing. In this, at least, Gertie had been correct. Pete Woodrow was not a man who would ever harm his daughter.

And if that was the case… "Amber, you said you told the father of your baby that you were pregnant ten days ago?"

"Yeah."

"Did he hurt you when you told him?"

"He...grabbed my wrists. And squeezed them, really hard. It hurt a lot. Like a burn, almost."

Pete swore. "What an asshole. Did he do anything else to you?"

"No. He let me go then. Told me it wasn't his baby and he never wanted to see me again."

Amber lowered her head again, as if with shame. Her father stepped forward and touched her chin gently. "He's the one who has no honor. You lift your head high, Daughter. You hear me?"

"Yes, Daddy."

Pete opened his arms and Amber stepped into her father's awkward embrace. The hug lasted only seconds, but Nadine sensed it was a breakthrough moment.

Pete wiped his eyes again. "Sounds like we need to get you to a doctor. And a counselor. Maybe we both should go to the counselor. I haven't been here for you. Drinking and wallowing in pity. It's time I stopped."

"Y-you're not mad at me?"

"You? Never."

Nadine quietly said good-bye and left. She'd check on Amber in another few weeks or so. For now, the young woman was in good hands.

✕

"I'VE GOT THE detective from Boston on the phone for you." Bea was in the doorway to Zak's office. She opened her mouth, as if to say more, but changed her mind and went back to her desk.

Zak didn't like to think his employees had to hold their tongues around him. He'd been silenced by Sheriff Ford too many times to do the same with his team. He made a note to ask Bea what she'd wanted to say later. It could be something innocuous, like should she order more toner for the printer. On the other hand, it could be a small detail that made all the difference to a case.

He picked up his phone. "Sheriff Zak Waller here."

"Detective Kane, eighth precinct Boston. How're things going in Montana?"

"They've been better. We've got a possible abducted child and a missing female adult. Freak snowstorm last night isn't helping."

"Snow in May? That's what you get for living in the mountains. I hear you had some questions about an old case from 1980?"

"That's right. My missing female lived in Boston at that time and I'm wondering if a man from her past might be involved in her disappearance. His name is Russell Graves. Back in 1980 she lived with him in Boston along with their infant daughter Jessica. The daughter died of smoke inhalation at age one. Manner of death was listed as homicide."

The detective whistled. "That's a long time ago. You got

social security numbers?"

"Not for the man. I do for Sybil and Jessica." He relayed them. "But that's all I got."

"It's a good start. I'll let you know what I find."

Bea was back in his office right after he hung up the phone.

"You got a minute?" She planted her hands on her hips.

Guess she wasn't too shy to speak up after all. "Yup."

"I'm all for finding out what happened to Sybil. But we've got a missing little girl. Don't you think we should be focusing on Darby right now?"

"That's what I'm doing, Bea."

She narrowed her eyes. "I hope you're on the right track with this."

"Believe me, so do I."

They were interrupted by the sound of the main door opening. Boots stomped on the mat, then Nadine called out.

"Pete Woodrow is home, safe and sound and recovering from a whopper of a hangover. Anything new here?"

"A forty-year-old photo album," Bea muttered, on her way back to her desk. "Go talk to the sheriff. He'll tell you all about it."

A few minutes later, Nadine came into his office with a coffee and a muffin. Cheeks still flushed from the cold outside, she settled in one of the visitor chairs that faced his desk. "What's this about a photo album?"

"Hang on a sec." He raised his voice. "Bea, did you upload that baby album into our evidence file?"

"Yes, boss."

"Mind bringing me the original?"

Bea brought the album and dropped it on his desk.

Frowning, Nadine watched Bea walk away. "What's wrong with her?"

"She thinks I'm barking up the wrong tree with this." Before handing her the album he asked, "Everything okay with the Woodrows?"

"I think so. I'll fill you in on the details later."

"How were the roads?"

"Terrible. It's stopped snowing, but thanks to the wind, visibility sucks and there're lots of packed snowdrifts."

"Hopefully the wind calms by tomorrow or that FBI agent won't be happy." He passed her the album.

Nadine's brow wrinkled as she studied the cover.

"This is a baby book."

"I found it wrapped in a quilt at the bottom of the chest in Sybil's bedroom."

Nadine opened the book to the first page and, eyes widening, sucked in her breath. "Sybil had a daughter?"

Zak leaned back in his chair, letting her draw her own conclusions. As the photos progressed over time, she too noticed the child's disability.

"There's something wrong. The baby should be sitting up. Crawling. Walking. She's not developing like a normal child would."

"I've been searching the internet for disabilities like that. One possibility that came up was cerebral palsy."

"I've met people with CP. I've never seen any of them look so…limp and listless."

"Yeah, it must be something else. Something we haven't heard of." At one time Zak would have asked Clark Pittman. But the former doctor had changed a lot in the past few years. He was no longer someone Zak trusted, as a doctor, or a person.

When Nadine reached the last page with pictures, she glanced at him. "Is this all?"

He nodded.

Nadine frowned, then her hands flew to the sides of her face. "Oh, no. The baby must have died. Whatever her disability was, it must have been fatal."

"She did die. But not of her disability." He pointed out the relevant lines on the death certificate. "Sounds like she died in a fire. Manner of death was ruled homicide."

Nadine flopped back in her chair. "But—who would kill a little baby?"

Zak told her about his conversation with Detective Kane from Boston. "I'm hoping he'll be in touch soon with some answers to that question. I'm guessing those answers will involve Russell Graves. If I'm correct on that, he could be the author of that anonymous letter to Sybil."

"What did the letter say exactly?"

Zak recited from memory. "*I want a second chance. You*

owe me."

"But it's been forty years. Why would he suddenly send her a message like this?"

Zak shrugged. "Maybe he was serving time and just got out? We'll know soon. I've got a guy in Boston checking into it for me."

Nadine switched back to the photo of the death certificate. "Jessica died on May the fifth. Zak, that's the date where Sybil drew all those little black hearts…no wonder she feels sad every spring."

"The baby book explains a lot of things. But I still don't understand why Sybil didn't tell anyone in Lost Trail about her relationship with Russell, or that they had a baby together."

"Forty years ago was it scandalous to have a baby without being married?"

"Forty years ago her parents were still alive. I suppose she could have been afraid of disappointing them. But it's a pretty big secret to keep."

"Easier when she was living on the other side of the country, I guess."

Zak's phone rang, breaking into their conversation. Zak grabbed the receiver. "Sheriff Zak Waller."

"Hey, Sheriff, this is Detective Kane again. I've got some information you're going to find very interesting."

"Hang on, I'll put you on speaker so Deputy Black can hear too." As he said this, Nadine got up to close the door to minimize outside noise.

"So," the detective began, "you asked me to check into the homicide of female baby Jessica Graves back in 1980. She died in a house fire that was set by her own father, that man being the Russell Graves you asked me to check into."

Zak and Nadine exchanged grim looks. "We were wondering if Graves was implicated in her death."

"He was and it gets worse. The Graves were living in the basement suite of the house. The couple who were renting the main level also died in the fire."

"Three homicides."

"Graves claimed he thought the couple were away on vacation. He said he spoke to them the previous day when they were loading suitcases into their car. He claimed they said they were planning to drive to upper New York state. This was never proven in court, though. The couple's car was found in their usual parking space the night of the fire. No suitcase in the truck."

"Graves set the fire on purpose?"

"Oh yes. He chose a day when his wife had evening classes at the university. Used gasoline-soaked rags that he placed on a pile of magazines in the middle of the baby's room. Graves didn't even try to deny it."

"But—why?" Nadine couldn't contain the most pressing question.

"Apparently the baby suffered from this rare defect. Spinal muscular atrophy," the detective said, articulating slowly and clearly as if he was reading the words directly from a report.

"I haven't heard of that." Nadine looked at Zak, and he shook his head. He hadn't either.

"Well, it's rare, I guess. And there are different levels of severity. The Graves baby had a pretty bad case. The medical expert for the trial said Jessica probably wouldn't have lived much beyond five years of age."

"But that's why Russell Graves killed her? Because of her condition?"

"He said he couldn't handle watching the little girl suffer. This SMA condition—it doesn't affect a child's personality or intelligence. So, this bright little baby was stuck in a body that didn't work. And it was taking a toll on the baby's mother. Graves testified he would wake up in the night and find Sybil crying. He just wanted all the pain to stop. And he couldn't think of another way."

Silence followed, as Zak absorbed the horror of the situation. Nadine looked just as shocked as he felt. Finally he was able to ask, "And did the court find Russell Graves guilty?"

"Hell yes. On three counts of intentional homicide as well as arson and some other things thrown in. His judge was very unsympathetic and gave him the maximum sentence for all his crimes." There was the sound of shuffling paper over the line, then the detective resumed speaking.

"You'll find this part especially relevant. Russell Graves was released from prison just three weeks ago."

Zak felt like pumping his fist in the air. Graves had to be their man. If he'd been in prison the past forty years, it would explain why he'd waited so long to send that message to Sybil. The kidnapping of Darby might also fit in, if he took her as some sort of replacement for their dead child. Jessica had been fair-haired and delicate. Maybe that was why Darby had been targeted?

"Was Graves permitted to travel outside the state of Massachusetts?" Conditions of parole usually restricted travel to within a specified area.

"He was not. But Graves missed his first scheduled meeting with his parole officer, so who knows where the hell he is. We have a warrant out for his arrest."

"Can you tell us anything else about Graves, Detective? His background, education, work experience?"

"Graves was born and raised in Boston. He studied librarian science in college. That's where he met your Sybil Tombe. I'll send you a current photo and a copy of the file. If he has abducted your missing woman and the child, I hope you find them quickly. This guy has been locked up a long, long time. And that can make a man kind of crazy."

Chapter Twenty-Four

"If Russell Graves has Sybil and Darby, I'd guess he's keeping them someplace relatively close. Within an hour or two drive from town," Zak estimated.

After days of following procedures that led nowhere, Zak finally felt in control of the investigation. He should have listened to his instincts about that teddy bear earlier. Possibly Darby's kidnapping could have been prevented.

"How can you know that?"

Nadine was munching on an apple again. She'd tossed one his way, but he'd set it aside on his desk. His sense of urgency about this case had never been higher. If he was right, if Russell Graves was their kidnapper, who knew what screwy intentions he might have in mind. Detective Kane was correct. They needed to find Sybil and Darby as soon as humanly possible.

"After Sybil was kidnapped, we know our perp came back to town on at least three different occasions. Once he was spotted at the school during recess. The next day Debbie-Ann saw him in the park."

"And the third time was when he kidnapped Darby."

"Exactly. All those trips back and forth to Lost Trail were risky. It only works if he had Sybil hidden somewhere reasonably close."

Nadine threw away her apple core—in the proper trash can this time—and grabbed a second apple. Zak couldn't understand how she could eat at a time like this. He went to the topo map on the wall. If he was looking for a good hideout...where would he go?

"Here's another question." Nadine came up beside him. "I can see why Graves might target Sybil. All that time in prison, he could have obsessed on her and created some sort of fantasy about how they would be together again when he was released. But why would he take Darby?"

"Darby is meant to replace the daughter they lost. Granted, she's a lot older than Jessica was when she died, but babies and toddlers are a lot of work, and more difficult to kidnap. In his mind, his daughter would be older by now anyway."

"Forty years old, in fact. Not eight."

"Yeah, well, logic, I'm guessing, is not going to be Russell Graves's strong suit."

He turned back to the map. "Search and rescue went door to door after Darby went missing. I can't believe we'll find them anywhere in town."

"How about the ski hill? Now that the season is over, the place is practically deserted."

"I sent Kenny out there this morning. Lots of potential

hiding spots. The lodge, the condos, the single-use chalets…"

"I'll go check in with him. See if he needs any help."

After Nadine left the room, Zak traced a finger along the borders of his county. Ravalli to the north, Deer Lodge to the east, Beaverhead to the south, and the state of Idaho to the west. The land along all these borders was the most vulnerable. Low population and rural, often in geologically challenging terrain.

A man who knew his way around rough mountain roads, who'd planned ahead and bought a trailer and a generator, he could live a long time without being noticed. He'd need to stock a bunch of food and fuel for the generator. Theoretically, it could be done.

But a library science major from Boston who'd spent the past forty years in prison didn't seem the kind of guy who'd have the right skill set for that.

No, more likely Russell had found himself a nice abandoned home. One of the ski chalets would be ideal, frankly.

He leaned out his door into the bullpen. "Nadine, did you get a hold of Kenny?"

"Just talked to him. He hasn't seen anything suspicious yet. He's been going door to door and figures he'll be finished in about an hour."

Up near the main door, behind the reception desk, Bea had been talking quietly on the phone. She hung up with a sigh. "Another bear-eating-garbage complaint from that old guy who lives year-round at Loon Lake. I told him we were tight for staff right now. Doesn't he follow the news? You'd think everyone in the county would realize a little girl's been kidnapped."

Zak stared at Bea. Was this it? Had it been under his nose the entire time? "What did Gregory Mondale say exactly?"

"Just that the same cinnamon-colored, black bear got into the garbage again last night. Same homeowners seem to be the culprit—35559 Lakeview Crescent."

"Yup. That's the house where I found all the garbage when I was out there last week," Nadine said. "They hadn't shut the bear-proof latch properly. I left a notice in their mailbox. This time I'll give them a fine."

Zak was getting that pre-run feeling again. Head buzzing, body tensed and ready to spring. This couldn't be a coincidence. "Nadine, let's drive out there right now."

Bea looked annoyed. "Isn't a nuisance bear low on the priority list right now?"

"The bear isn't the priority. It's the people creating the garbage."

A BIT OF heaven tucked into the Bitterroot Valley, that was Loon Lake. Turquoise waters surrounded by a majestic, centuries-old ponderosa pine forest. Zak liked to slip out before the summer people came to go running on the path that circumnavigated the lake. Three sides of the path were set above the lake on forty-foot cliffs, but at the north end of the lake the land leveled off.

This was where you found the cottages. On the northeast corner were the old-timers, people who had built modest structures in the fifties and sixties. Most were summer use only, but Gregory Mondale had moved out here permanently after he retired from the US Forest Service.

Zak liked checking in with Gregory now and then. He could always be counted on for updates on activity in the area.

He drove to Gregory's cottage now, a small A-frame with a separate garage. Zak figured this was a good opportunity to introduce Nadine. Some of the older folks who'd been born in the Bitterroot Valley tended to be skeptical of outsiders, even those from other parts of Montana.

"Gregory can seem standoffish, but he's a good guy. Not much happens around here that he doesn't notice."

They got out of the sheriff-mobile at almost the same time, their doors shutting within a second of each other. The elevation at the lake was lower than in town and they hadn't had as much snow here. Just six inches or so.

Smoke puffed from Mondale's chimney; boot tracks had worn a path from the side door to the woodpile. Clearly Gregory was home.

He came to the door before they knocked, a broad-shouldered man who stood at least three inches above six feet.

"Zak. Didn't think our garbage situation warranted a visit from the sheriff."

"Right now, I'm more concerned about a missing eight-year-old girl and our town librarian than I am about a bear. Have you met our new deputy? Nadine Black, this is Gregory Mondale."

The two shook hands.

"Yeah, I heard the Amber Alert on the radio," Gregory said. "What's going on?"

"We've got a suspect. And I'm wondering if he's using one of the vacant summer cottages."

"Ah. You think he's the one leaving out the garbage?"

Zak and Nadine were still standing on the large mat by the side door. Gregory didn't often extend hospitality to uninvited guests. In this case it was just as well, because Zak didn't want to waste time.

"Maybe. But Deputy Black was out here last Thursday. She said she knocked on the door at 35559 and no one seemed to be around."

"A few folks were out for the weekend. I didn't see any lights at 35559 at night, though. And that's definitely the house with the garbage problem. This can't go on. That bear gets used to eating people garbage and he's going to hang around all summer. When bears and people mix, it's always the bear who ends up paying the price."

Zak knew what he meant. A bear habituated to garbage was considered a problem bear. Problem bears were sometimes relocated, but mostly they were shot.

"We'll go check it now," Zak promised. On his way out the door he paused. "The folks that were out for the weekend. Any of them driving dark-colored pickup trucks?"

"I've seen a few trucks like that around. Can you be more specific?"

Zak sighed. He wished.

NADINE COULD SENSE Zak's anticipation and it was making her edgy, almost nervous. As they drove to the northwest side of the lake where the upscale cottages were, she tried to distract herself.

"I don't think your friend Gregory likes me." He hadn't said a word to her, or even looked her way after their introduction.

"It's not a matter of liking. You want his respect. His trust. That's what counts." Zak pulled over to the side of the road, just behind the garbage bin belonging to house number 35559.

Nadine followed him out of the truck. Detritus from the bear's scavenging was everywhere. "Damn. I cleaned this up last time I was here."

"The garbage lid isn't fastened correctly."

"Wasn't last time either. I left a note."

He followed her to the side entrance, where her note was still stuffed between the door and the frame.

"I guess they don't use this door much."

Zak knocked. When no one answered, he led the way to the lakefront side of the property. This side of the house was almost entirely windows, closed off with blinds. He knocked on the patio doors, several times, but there was still no response.

Nadine turned from the house to the lake. "This is where I saw those loons."

The wind was raising some good-sized waves. Not good fishing weather, for people or birds.

"Let's go back to the main road." Once there, Zak looked up and down the street. "You know what? If I was in hiding, I'd probably leave my garbage in front of someone else's house."

Nadine considered this a moment. "Makes sense. Want to split up? We'll make better time that way."

"This guy is armed and probably desperate. Let's go together."

ZAK AND NADINE spent an hour knocking on doors and peering in windows.

The majority of the cottages were vacant. In three cases,

though, someone came to the door when they knocked. Each had their own reasons for being up at the lake this time of year.

A man in his twenties was working on a thesis; a middle-aged man who smelled like beer had just separated from his wife; and an annoyed-looking woman with her hair in a ponytail owned her own cleaning company and was doing spring cleaning.

They encountered the acrid smell of burned food at the cottage at the end of the crescent-shaped road. The house was set back amid the trees, with a long lane that eventually led to a double garage attached by a causeway to a classic, Montana-style log home with a green metal roof.

"Smells like burning cheese," Nadine guessed.

They'd left the sheriff-mobile on the road and were walking up the lane. Zak studied the windows. As with most of the other homes, the blinds were all shut. The snow outside the cottage was pristine. No one had walked or driven here since the snow stopped this morning.

As with the other places, they walked the perimeter of the home first, hoping to find a window with an open blind or some other clue about potential occupants. Every few steps they stopped to listen.

At the back of the house, Zak thought he could hear music. Nadine heard it too. She moved to the casement window at the foundation of the home, put a finger to her pursed lips and removed her hat. After about thirty seconds she stood tall. A knowing spark lit up her blue eyes. "That's a song from the *Lion King* movie. I bet someone's watching a DVD down there."

He gave a slow nod. That someone could be Darby. As probable cause, it was weak. But the stakes were too high for him to worry about protecting his ass. "We're going in."

The front door was a formidable hunk of solid wood, but the door off the back deck was mostly window with a fir frame. Not only that, the wood looked weathered and cracked in places. He guessed it would collapse with one good shoulder check.

"Ready?" He took out his gun and waited until Nadine had done the same. He made a fist and pounded three times.

"Sheriff department. Open up now."

From inside he heard a loud metallic squeak—an oven door?—then the sound of panicked footsteps. Zak yelled out one more warning, then threw his body at the door. As he'd guessed, the wooden frame cracked, and then the glass shattered.

Zak used his back—thickly padded with his jacket—to push through the rest of the glass. Once inside, he scanned the room. No one here. It was the kitchen. The oven door was open, and a blackened pizza was splattered on the hardwood floor.

He could hear Nadine breathing hard behind him. "You okay?"

"Yup. Let's go!"

Zak followed the sound of heavy footsteps. Down the hall. Past a huge oil painting of a bear. Around a corner. And…there he was.

Chapter Twenty-Five

Russell Graves jabbed desperately at the dead bolt lock on the door to the basement, but his hands were shaking. He couldn't fit the key in fast enough.

"Raise your hands," Zak shouted, leveling his Glock at the man, heart center. To his left, Nadine mirrored his actions.

"I'm Sheriff Waller and this is Deputy Black. We're looking for Sybil Tombe and Darby Larkin. We'd appreciate your cooperation, Mr. Graves."

The man froze at the sound of his name. He stopped struggling with the key and turned, eyes wide, incredulous. He must not have expected to be identified. His eyes flashed from Zak to Nadine, then back again. And then his shoulders slumped, and the key slipped out of his fingers to the floor.

"Hands up," Zak repeated.

Slowly the man complied.

Behind him, the door to the basement was shaking and creaking as someone on the other side pulled desperately on the knob. "Help! Help! Is someone out there? Please help us!"

"We're coming, Sybil," Zak called. "Give us a minute and we'll unlock the door."

Up close Russell Graves did not smell good. His hair and beard were long and unkempt. He'd bulked up from the days when he and Sybil had lived in Boston. Mostly muscle. But there was no fight in the man as he gazed down the barrel of Nadine's 38 Special.

"Russell Graves." Zak's jaw was clenched so hard he could barely get out the words. "I'm placing you under arrest." He would read him his rights in a few minutes. Now he just needed the man immobilized.

He cuffed Grave's bony wrists behind his back while Nadine kept her gun trained on the perp. Once the cuffs were secured, he nodded at Nadine. "Okay. You can unlock the door now."

Nadine grabbed the key from the floor and made short work of the job.

The door flung open and Sybil, dragging Darby by the hand, stepped out of the basement.

"Oh, thank God," she murmured. Then her arms dropped to her sides and she collapsed to her knees.

"Sybil, are you okay?" Nadine crouched by the older woman and took her hand.

"I-I'm so relieved. My legs just gave out on me."

Darby peeked out from behind Sybil, and Zak mustered what he hoped was a reassuring smile. "Hey, Darby. Remember me? I came to the café to talk to you and your mom."

Darby nodded but didn't speak. She didn't appear to have been physically hurt. Her clothing was tidy and her hair neatly brushed and braided. The expression in her deep-set gray eyes, however, bordered on terror as she stared, transfixed, at the man in handcuffs.

"You're safe now," Zak promised her. "We're going to phone your mom and dad. You'll be able to see them soon."

"H-he kidnapped me!" Darby finally said, pointed at Russell Graves.

"No, no, it wasn't like that. Tell them, Sybil. I didn't hurt anyone. I never wanted to hurt anyone." Leaning against the wall, Graves looked unsteady on his feet. Hands fastened behind his back played havoc on the body's sense of balance.

Sybil didn't answer, refused to even look in the prisoner's direction. With Nadine's help, she got back on her feet and held out her arms to Darby. "We're safe now, honey. I told you they would find us."

Darby stepped into the librarian's hug. Zak got the impression Sybil had done a lot of reassuring during the twenty-four hours Darby had spent in captivity.

"You're both okay?" Nadine asked. "Any injuries?"

"Once he got us here, he didn't touch us," Sybil said. "We had lots of food and water. So, yes, *physically* we're fine."

Mentally Zak triaged all the work to be done. Being this far from town didn't help. "Nadine, call Bea and have her get Kenny out here STAT. Then phone the Larkins and let them know their daughter is safe."

"Will do, Sheriff." Nadine's eyes shone with tears. He had a good idea how she was feeling. But for now, he was keeping a lid on his emotions. There was a lot to do.

Next on the list was getting Graves safely secured in the back seat of the sheriff-mobile. Quietly he instructed Nadine on what to say to Bea and the Larkins, then with his gun he gestured toward the hallway. "Let's go, Graves."

"You don't understand. I was doing this for Sybil. Tell them, babe. You know I did it all for you." When she didn't respond, he implored Zak. "You have to listen to my side of the story."

"I'll make you a deal," Zak said. "I'll tell you my story now and you can tell me yours when we're at my office." He gave the man a helpful push toward the door and began reciting his rights.

IN HER SHORT career as deputy, Nadine had never been involved in anything this intense. Her body buzzed as if she'd had a triple espresso, but her insides felt empty, hollowed out like she'd suffered a terrible loss.

She hated to think of how scared Sybil and Darby must

have been. Thank God the ordeal was over. Sybil and Darby seemed to be okay, and she and Zak hadn't been harmed in the takedown. If Graves had been armed with a gun, it all could have gone down much differently.

But the only weapon she'd seen during her mad dash through the kitchen was a six-inch hunting knife on the counter next to the stove. Graves must have put it down when he was trying to pull the burning pizza from the oven.

Once Zak removed Graves from the house, Sybil and Darby were visibly relieved.

"Let's sit over there for a bit." Nadine gestured to a room off the front entrance where comfy-looking leather furniture, draped with wool Pendleton blankets, was arranged around a massive stone fireplace.

Sybil and Darby went to the sofa and sat right next to each other, with Sybil still holding Darby's hand.

In an attempt to dispel the horror-movie atmosphere, Nadine opened the blinds. "That's better."

Sybil thanked her. "We haven't seen much daylight lately."

"When are my mom and dad going to get here?" Darby asked.

"They're going to meet you at the sheriff's office. I'll call in right now and get Deputy Bombard to come and pick you guys up."

No way would she and Zak drive the victims back in the same vehicle as the man who had abducted them.

Nadine had to explain the situation twice to Bea, who was so shocked she couldn't seem to absorb what had happened. Nadine didn't blame her. She felt a little stunned herself.

"Tell Kenny we need him right away at Loon Lake. And don't forget the evidence kit." She gave Bea the address, then dialed the Larkins.

Patsy answered the phone sounding breathless. "Hello?"

In that one word Nadine heard both hope and fear.

"Deputy Black here. Good news. We have Darby and Sybil. Both are fine. I'll put Darby on the line for a bit." Nadine handed her phone to the little girl.

"Mom?"

As soon as she heard her mother's voice, Darby started to cry. Soon she was blubbering so hard she couldn't get out a single word.

Sybil took the phone from the little girl's hand. "Patsy, she isn't hurt physically, she's just been through a lot, you know?"

Sybil listened as Patsy said something, then she lifted her gaze to Nadine. "She and Chris want to come and get Darby right away."

"Let me speak with them." Nadine reclaimed her phone. "We're still at the crime scene, Patsy. We don't want to contaminate any evidence. It's better if you pick Darby up at the sheriff's office. If Darby is up to it, we'd like to get her official statement before she goes home. You and Chris can be with her, of course. And though she looks fine, it would be good to get a doctor to look her over." She remembered last night's blizzard. "Once the pass opens up."

✕

IN THE END, Kenny stayed behind to process the crime scene, while Zak and Nadine drove back to Lost Trail in separate vehicles. Zak had the prisoner secured in the sheriff-mobile, while Nadine drove Kenny's truck, with Darby and then Sybil beside her on the bench seat.

"Kenny said he has an emergency stash of granola bars and water bottles if you want," Nadine offered.

"No, thanks," both Sybil and Darby said.

Sybil's wildly curly hair was cut in a short bob. She pushed the fringe off her forehead, exposing her weary-looking eyes. "I'm really not hungry, but I am looking forward to a good salad. All he fed us was frozen convenience food like pizza and burritos."

"And Oreo cookies and ripple potato chips. Stuff my mom never lets me eat."

It was good to hear Darby talking. Nadine wasn't a psychologist, but she guessed it was healthier than keeping silent and bottling up all her thoughts and emotions.

"We had to stay in the basement," Darby continued. "We couldn't even come up to eat our meals."

"The owners of the house had a nice entertainment system and a big collection of children-appropriate movies, books and board games. They provided very good distraction."

"The crazy man said we were a family and we had to stay together forever. That scared me. But when we were alone Sybil explained it wasn't true. She said someone would rescue us, but until then we had to pretend to agree with him. We had to do that, or else he might get angry and do something…bad."

"He is a very mentally disturbed man," Nadine agreed. "Good thing he's going back to prison where he won't be able to hurt or scare any more people."

"I can't wait to see Mom and Dad and even Trevor. Mom's going to be mad though. I'm not supposed to go in the forest. Not even a few steps."

"Your mom is going to be so happy you're safe. I guarantee she won't be angry."

"Do you know what happened to the dog? He was crying and I tried to help him. But then the crazy guy came out of the woods with his knife. He covered my mouth and said if I screamed, he would cut me and then kill the dog."

"The dog is fine. His name is Alfred and he belongs to Gertie Humphrey. If you ever want to see him, you just need to go to the convenience store at the gas station."

"Oh, good. You were right, Sybil. The crazy guy didn't hurt him."

Sybil had been a godsend to Darby, Nadine could see.

She'd shielded the young girl, given her hope, and distracted her with games and stories and movies.

But no one had been in that house to shield or protect Sybil. Even now while she was keeping up a brave front for the young girl's sake, her dull eyes betrayed her emotional bruises, and her lips sagged with exhaustion.

Nadine noticed her rubbing her forehead. She'd done this a few times now. Maybe she had a headache.

"Want to grab some painkillers from Kenny's first aid kit?"

"That's okay."

About an hour into the drive Darby went from relaying a story Sybil had read to her that morning, to falling fast asleep, her head leaning on Sybil's shoulder.

"Poor girl is exhausted. She didn't sleep much last night. I told her stories and tried to comfort her as much as I could. But it was a terrifying situation."

"You must be exhausted too."

"I feel like I could sleep for a week. If only I could block out everything that happened." Sybil was rubbing her forehead again.

It wasn't because of pain, Nadine realized. She was trying to rub out the memories. Not just the bad ones from this week. But the even worse ones from forty years ago.

"What was it like for you before Darby arrived?" Nadine asked quietly.

"Terrifying, of course. But not uncomfortable. Most of

the time I was in the entertainment room in the basement. Russell would sit with me. He did a lot of talking. Rambling. I suppose in a way, he was purging his soul. We were a couple once, you see. Back when we were young."

"Yes. Zak figured that out. He also found out about Russell Graves's criminal history—and about your daughter. I'm so sorry, Sybil."

The older woman turned to look out the passenger window. Nadine was sure she didn't take in a bit of their surroundings. Several minutes went by before she spoke again.

"In his twisted mind, Russ was trying to turn back the clock to the years when we were doctoral students, living simply, but so happy. He didn't—force himself on me. He said he knew it would take time for me to love him again."

"He thought you might do that? Love him again?"

Sybil shrugged. "I didn't try to argue. There was no point. I just hoped that if I made a show of being docile, he'd eventually relax enough to make a mistake. Leave the key where I could find it. Or forget his phone when he went upstairs to get food. Just one slipup was all I needed."

"What about when he left you alone so he could drive to town?"

"He'd lock me in the wine cellar. It wasn't terrible. I had water and snacks and books."

"Did you dip into the wine collection?"

Sybil smiled faintly. "I was tempted. But I wanted to

keep a clear head, in case I got a chance to escape. After the fifth night, though, I was feeling sort of hopeless. And then Russ left and came back with Darby. I almost lost my mind. I couldn't believe he'd kidnapped a totally innocent young girl. That's when I realized he was completely insane."

"Can I ask one more question, Sybil? Zak noticed a teddy bear on your kitchen counter. Was it your daughter's?"

"Yes. I kept it on my bed. Russ saw it there and brought it out to the kitchen. He told me he meant to bring it with us but he forgot."

Nadine was about to reply, when she noticed Sybil had started to tremble. "Are you okay?"

"Could you turn up the heat? I feel cold."

Nadine gave her another sharp look. "You're going into delayed shock. Hang on a minute." She eased the vehicle to a stop then pulled a blanket and an energy bar from the space behind the seat. She'd have to thank Kenny later for keeping his truck so well stocked.

She tucked the blanket around Sybil and Darby—the little girl sighed but didn't awaken—and Nadine gave Sybil the bar. "Eat this. You need the sugar."

"I'm sorry, I'm not sure what came over me."

"You were kidnapped by your ex, Sybil, and held prisoner for six days. You're entitled to a little shock."

Chapter Twenty-Six

DARBY'S PARENTS WERE waiting on the street outside the sheriff's office when Nadine pulled into Kenny's parking space.

Chris Larkin opened the passenger door as soon as the truck stopped. Darby scrambled over Sybil's lap. "Daddy! Mommy!"

Chris lifted her safely to the sidewalk. "You're really here. You're safe. Oh, thank God."

"My baby girl!" Patsy cried as she threw her arms around her daughter. Even Trevor, standing with teenaged diffidence next to his family, had to rub a tear from his eye.

"Glad you're home, kid," he said to his sister.

"Get in here, Son," his father said. And soon all four Larkins were engulfed in the family hug.

Nadine put her hand on Sybil's shoulder as they watched the Larkins' joyful reunion. When they finally pulled apart, Sybil said, "I'm so sorry, Patsy and Chris. I know these past two days have been a parent's worst nightmare."

"And why should you be sorry?" Patsy left her daughter's side long enough to give the librarian a hug. "You're a victim, too. I'm so glad you're home now. Safe and sound."

Nadine checked with Bea, to make sure Russell was safely out of sight in the lockup, before she ushered everyone up the stairs and into the office. Bea had arranged for Farrah Saddler, a local nurse, to examine Darby and Sybil.

Farrah concluded that both appeared fine, though she cautioned the shock and exhaustion would take time to wear off.

"Is it okay if we get Darby's statement now?" Zak asked the parents.

Chris nodded, but Patsy shook her head. "I just want to take her home."

"Maybe it's better to get it over with." Chris turned to his daughter. "Are you okay to tell the sheriff what happened? Or do you want to go home and rest first?"

"I can tell him now," Darby said bravely.

Zak motioned for Nadine to join him and the family at the desk in his office. With her parents seated on either side of her, Darby repeated the things she'd told Nadine during the drive. When Zak asked about the day she'd been kidnapped, Darby confirmed she'd heard a dog crying through the open window.

"Did you open the window?" Zak asked.

"No. I thought Mom did."

Zak nodded, then glanced at Nadine who was sitting at his desk making notes. This confirmed he'd been right about the window being pried open from the outside. Really, Zak had been right about a lot of things, Nadine thought, as she watched him guide Darby through her statement.

Nadine craved a coffee. Instead, she took an apple from the bowl on Zak's desk and listened as Darby described the drive out to Loon Lake. The crazy man had tied her hands together and made her sit on the floor next to the passenger seat. He'd told her he was taking her to meet her new mother. Then he didn't speak for the rest of the drive.

"I was really scared until he took me into the house. When I saw Ms. Tombe, I knew I'd be okay. She kept me safe."

"Okay," Zak said after twenty minutes of questions and answers. "We'll write up all this into a victim's statement and bring it by your house tomorrow. Right now, I think Darby needs to go home."

As they got up to leave, the Larkins thanked him and Nadine profusely.

And then it was Sybil's turn. Bea had been taking care of her in the bullpen, plying her with herbal tea and Harvey's muffins.

"I'm sure this is the last thing you feel like doing, Sybil." Zak looked at the librarian sympathetically. "But it's best to do it now, while the details are fresh."

"Like I'd ever forget."

"I'll make it as painless as possible." He gestured for her to take the chair Darby had just vacated. Nadine sat on the other side with the recorder.

"Now. Please tell us what happened Thursday, May second, starting from when you left the library at six."

Sybil described going to the store to buy ingredients for her dinner. "When I came home, I let myself in the front door as usual. I was in a hurry to check my computer, so I set the groceries down with my purse and went to the office. But while I was on the computer, I heard a noise in the kitchen. The floor in there is very creaky.

"As soon as I saw the crossword and the orange peel on the table, I should have run. Russ always ate an orange when he was working on the weekend crossword."

"But you were caught off guard," Zak suggested.

"That's right. I hesitated too long. It wasn't until I noticed the teddy bear he'd put on the kitchen counter that I knew for sure it was Russ. I didn't see him though. He must have been standing behind the kitchen door. And then he must have had a drink in his hand, because I heard what sounded like glass breaking at the same time as he grabbed me."

"He was drinking some of the V8 juice you had in the fridge," Zak told her. "I saw the liquid on the floor from your kitchen window and assumed it was blood. What happened after he grabbed you?"

"It must have been some sort of chokehold, because I couldn't breathe. Everything went black and the next thing I knew, my hands were tied together, and so were my feet. I was in some sort of truck, wrapped up in blankets, and it felt like we were driving quickly over gravel roads."

"Russell did a lot of talking on our drive," Zak said. "He told me he'd heard some people talking in the post office about the Elliots and how they generally didn't show up at their summer cottage until July."

"Is that the family who own the house where he took us?"

"It is. Graves told me he figured it would take a few months for you to adjust to the idea of being a family again. And then you would sell your house in Lost Trail and move back to Boston with him."

"Oh, Lord." Sybil propped her elbow on the table and covered her eyes with one hand. After a few moments she'd collected herself enough to ask another question. "How did you find out about Russ, Zak? How did you know he was the one who'd kidnapped us?"

Zak went to his desk and pulled the baby album out of the bottom drawer. "I found this in the chest in your bedroom. Under all the quilts." He set the book gently in front of her. "I'm so sorry about your daughter."

Sybil bowed her head. And wept.

THERE WAS A strange truck parked in front of Sybil's house when Tiff and her mother showed up with cookies and flowers.

"Who could that be?" Rosemary peered into the window as they passed by.

Tiff took a look at the back of the truck. "The license starts with four, so whoever it is comes from Missoula County."

Sybil opened the door before they knocked. She looked fragile and tired, but happy to see them.

"My friend." Rosemary passed the tin of cookies to Tiff so she could engulf Sybil in a hug. "I'm so happy to have you back."

"Me too." Tiff handed her the flowers and tin of cookies. "What a terrible ordeal you've been through."

Kenny had called shortly after lunch to let them know Sybil and Darby had been found and were safe. Since then she and her mom had been waiting for Sybil to get home so they could see for themselves that she was okay.

"I'm very grateful to be here. And to have good friends who care."

"I'm afraid I haven't cared enough over the years," Rosemary said frankly. "When Zak told us about everything that happened to you in Boston, I didn't believe him at first. I hate to think that you suffered through all of that alone. That I was too preoccupied with my own problems to be there for you."

"That's my fault. I tried to box up that part of my past and pretend it never happened. But enough talking at the front door. Come in. There's someone I want you to meet."

A nice-looking gentleman with trendy dark glasses and a goatee was seated in the living room. He stood as Sybil made introductions.

"Jeffery Taylor, I'd like you to meet my dearest friend, Rosemary Masterson, and her daughter Tiffany."

After they'd all said hello, Tiff and her mother sat in the armchairs, leaving the sofa for Sybil and Jeffery.

Sybil cleared her throat. "I'm glad you're all together. I want to tell you about my past—about my daughter Jessica—and it will be easier to only have to say it once."

Rosemary nodded and leaned forward, ready to listen.

"I got pregnant when I was doing my postdoc in Boston. I didn't tell anyone back home because I knew my parents would disapprove, especially my mother who was a by-the-book Catholic."

"She was awfully strict," Rosemary recalled.

"Yes. And they were already pretty upset that I'd decided to go to school across the country. I knew there was no risk they'd ever come to visit…so I just kept quiet. Denial is no solution, but I was young and perhaps not the wisest in that regard."

"Was Russell Graves the father?" Rosemary asked.

"Yes. We'd met in a class on…heck, I can't remember which class it was…the important thing is that we'd only been dating a few months when I got pregnant. I wasn't sure I wanted to marry Russ, but we did move in together after Jessica was born. And things went okay, at first. But a few weeks after the birth, or maybe a month, I started to worry. Jessica was just so placid. When I took her to the clinic, or out for walks, I'd notice other babies. They all seemed to wiggle and move their heads a lot more than Jessica. According to the books I read, she should have been rolling over at four months and sitting at six. She did neither."

"Oh, Sybil."

Jeffery reached for her hand. Sybil gave a brave smile. And continued.

"I'd been sharing my concerns with the doctor at the baby clinic. And it was around this time that they finally figured out what was going on. My baby, my sweet Jessica, had spinal muscular atrophy. It's a hereditary disease that causes weakness and wasting of voluntary muscles. There are three types. Jessica's was Type II."

"It wasn't treatable? Curable?" Jeffery asked gently.

"Some types are treatable, but not Jessica's. SMA is never curable. We were warned her life span would be short. She would probably never have made it to the age of six."

Tiff couldn't stop her tears, didn't even want to. They were all crying. Sybil left the room for a moment and came back with a box of tissues.

"The especially cruel thing about SMA is that it doesn't affect a baby's brain. Jessica was intelligent. As she grew older, I would read to her and I could tell she understood. She loved when I took her for walks. At the park, I'd sit on the swing with her and rock gently back and forth and she would giggle so much. She was such a delightful child…but she could hardly move her body at all. Even eating could be hard for her."

"Oh Sybil," murmured Jeffery.

"Sometimes when we were around other babies and toddlers, I would see her watching them and even though she was so young I could tell she knew something was wrong with her. She'd look at me with such pleading in her eyes. *Momma, help.* Those were her very first words."

Sybil grabbed more tissues. "I would have given anything if she could just reach for her favorite teddy bear. Or hold her arms out for a hug. But Jessica was never able to do either of those things. Let alone sit and crawl and walk like other babies."

"Poor little girl." Tiff had known the pain of loving a brother who had not been expected to live to become an adult. At least Casey had been able to walk and run and live a mostly normal life during his twelve years on earth.

"What an evil disease." Rosemary grabbed a second tissue from the box. "I wonder why I've never heard of it?"

"It's rare. A baby has to inherit two faulty genes, one from each parent. So, it was just…tragic bad luck."

"I'm so sorry, Sybil." Rosemary left her chair to give her friend a hug.

"Yes, it was hard," Sybil said. "But there was happiness, too. Jessica loved music and stories and being outside. I desperately wanted her to have as much time and as much love as humanly possible. But her father saw the situation very differently."

"How did Russell cope with having a severely handicapped child?"

"Badly. He spent more time at the university, less at home. He didn't like talking about Jessica or our situation, and I was too focused on my baby to draw him out. So, his issues festered, and the distance between us grew, but I never guessed that he had reached the stage where he might be a danger. If I had, I never would have left Jessica alone with him. Never."

"Of course, you wouldn't," Rosemary said. "But how could you have guessed?"

"I should have seen signs. Russ would talk so fondly about our life before the baby. Once he asked our doctor if there were care facilities for babies like Jessica. I shot that idea down fast. Russ insisted he was only thinking of me. How tired and stressed I was. I failed to see that he hadn't bonded with our daughter. Not at all."

Sybil paused and Tiff wrapped her arms around her torso, tensing for what was coming next.

Jeffery stroked Sybil's back. "You don't have to tell us any more. You've already been through so much."

"Thank you, Jeffery, but I need to say this now or I might never again find the strength. I want the people closest to me to finally know my story. But it might be easier with a glass of scotch. There's a bottle in the cabinet over the fridge.

Jeffery, do you mind?"

"Not at all."

Jeffery went to the kitchen and returned with a bottle and four glasses. He poured a generous shot in each and handed them out.

Sybil took a sip. Then a deep breath. "Jessica was sixteen months old the day I kissed her for the last time. I'd been teaching a night class since January, so we were in a routine. I would put Jessica to bed, and Russ would work at the kitchen table. It was the easiest babysitting gig going since Jessica almost always slept through the night."

Sybil paused for a second sip. "On this night, however, May the fifth, Russ had a plan. I didn't find out about this until later in court when he told the judge he'd seen the couple who lived on the main floor of our house—we rented the basement suite—packing their car for a holiday. So, he took a month's worth of newspaper into Jessica's bedroom—he'd been saving them—and added all our books and old research papers to the pile, as well as our wooden kitchen chairs. Then he dumped a gallon of gasoline over all of it, lit a match and left. He just turned his back on our sleeping baby…and left."

"No," Rosemary said. "Oh, dear God, no."

Tiff took a good long swallow of the scotch. So, did everyone else.

"It so happened that the couple living above us had decided to leave for their holiday the next morning. They died in the fire too. Russ went to prison for forty years, and I moved back to Lost Trail. I told everyone I had completed my doctorate program, but that was a lie."

Sybil was glossing over the worst period of her life in just a couple of sentences. Tiff could understand why.

"I was so grateful I hadn't told anyone about Russ or Jessica. That meant I could shelve those years in the back of my mind and pretend they never happened. I had my emotions so locked up, I couldn't even invite my closest friends into my house."

"I feel so self-centered," Rosemary said. "If I hadn't been so wrapped up in my problems, you might have felt you could talk to me about yours."

"Don't blame yourself, my friend. I didn't want to talk to anyone. It was my choice. As the years went by, I began to heal, sort of. I started to enjoy life, not just go through the motions, as I reconnected with my old friends. But the deepest part of me stayed separate and aloof. Jeffery even commented on it after we'd been dating for about a month."

"I thought you enjoyed my company as much as I enjoy yours. We definitely have so much in common. But I felt you were holding back emotionally," Jeffery said. "I never guessed you had such a terrible loss in your past."

"This past week has been a nightmare, but I'm hoping something good comes from it. I don't want to keep my friends at arm's length anymore."

"And I want to be there for you when you need me,"

Rosemary said. "Now I hope you don't mind me asking…but do you have any pictures of Jessica? I'd love to see them."

It was the perfect question to have asked. Sybil's answering smile was both shy and proud. "Her baby book is on the dining room table."

They took turns exclaiming over the precious photographs. Jessica had been a round-faced, snub-nosed cutie with adorable dimples in her pudgy cheeks. As she grew older, there was no denying the intelligent sparkle in her eyes. And it grew more painful to see how trapped she was in her uncooperative body.

All too soon they reached the end of the book. Sybil closed it, then hugged it to her chest. "My only comfort is that the medical examiner said she died of smoke inhalation. She wouldn't have suffered for long. Perhaps she never even woke up."

Sybil took a deep, cleansing breath. "I think that's enough talking for one day. If you don't mind, my dear friends, I need to lie down for a while." She reached for Jeffery's hand. "You'll stay?"

"I'd be happy to."

Tiff and Rosemary gave Sybil a hug, with promises to get together soon, then Jeffery walked them to the front door.

"It was a pleasure to meet you," Rosemary said.

"And you," Jeffery said as he shook their hands. "I hope I get to see you both soon. Sounds like Sybil is a few decades behind in hosting dinner parties."

Sybil laughed at that. "Yes. Next gathering is definitely at my place."

As they walked toward their car, Tiff's mom said, "My poor, dear friend. She's been through so much. But isn't Jeffery a gem? You can tell how much he cares for her."

"I agree." She gave her mom a small hip bump. "Maybe you should give Montana Matches a try, too."

Chapter Twenty-Seven

NADINE WAS ON her third apple of the night, when Zak finally clued in. He stopped midsentence in the report he was writing and stared through his open door into the bullpen. He sat frozen for several minutes as the life he'd imagined for himself—and for Nadine—went through a major script change.

Could he do it? Was he capable?

The joy bubbling in his chest gave him his answer.

He saved his document and shut down his computer.

It was past midnight and only he and Nadine were still in the office. Weeks and weeks of documenting the evidence to build the case against Russell Graves remained, but the urgent stuff was taken care of. They'd scoured the Loon Lake house for evidence, which Kenny would be taking to the lab tomorrow. They'd obtained witness statements, delivered a progress report to the FBI, reported Russell Graves's arrest to Boston, and arranged to transport Russell Graves to the Montana State Prison.

Everything else could wait for tomorrow.

He stared at the bowl of apples Nadine had put on his

desk last week. Only two remained. Then he went to the bullpen. She glanced at him, smiled, then continued working on her notes. He went behind her and placed his hands on her shoulders.

"I'm clocking 'off' as sheriff and 'in' as your boyfriend. Would you like a shoulder massage?"

"You never need to ask me that. Always assume the answer is yes."

He admired Nadine's strong shoulders and long, graceful neck. This would be more fun if she wasn't wearing her regulation shirt, but at least she'd removed her shoulder harness. "We haven't had time to talk about what happened with the Woodrows this morning."

"Wow. It feels so long ago now." Nadine dropped her pen and closed her eyes. "Um, this is really nice."

"The Woodrows?"

"Oh, right. Well, Pete went out drinking last night in the storm—not the smartest move—and ended up driving his truck into the ditch. He was still passed out when I found him, but he finally came to and let me drive him home."

"Amber must have been relieved."

"She was, but I could tell something else was bothering her and she finally told me what it was. She's six months pregnant. The guy who made her that way is being a jerk and she was afraid how her father was going to react. So she hadn't told him. Or anyone else."

"Crap. Poor kid."

"I was wrong about her dad, though. I thought he was abusive, but I was way off base about him. He overheard Amber and me talking, and he wasn't angry at all. He apologized for having checked out as a father. He promised Amber he'd get her to a doctor and a therapist. He even said he would go for therapy too, so hopefully he'll get help with his drinking problem."

"Were you surprised?"

"About what?" She twisted in her chair so she could look him in the eyes. He took her hands and pulled up, so they were standing face-to-face.

"Amber being pregnant."

"Well…not really."

"I wondered why you had such a connection to Amber. Why you seemed to care so much. I've been wondering other things, too. Like whether you were pulling back from me, questioning our relationship."

"If I've seemed different, it has nothing to do with my feelings for you. Your job and responsibilities are a challenge, but I wouldn't want to be with any other guy."

"Even though I've been such an idiot? I should have realized what was going on so much sooner. I mean apples? Since when do you eat apples instead of drinking coffee?"

A small smile tugged at one corner of Nadine's beautiful mouth and a stain of pink rose up from the pale skin of her neck.

Zak took both as confirmation he was right. "When did

you find out?"

"Two weeks ago."

He touched his lips to her forehead. "And I thought being elected sheriff was a life changer."

"Pretty shocking, huh?"

"I guess. But in a good way."

"You sure? I was afraid, with your childhood..."

"It was rough. But I've never been anything like my father. Are you scared I won't make a good dad?"

"Of course not. Mostly I was scared you didn't want to be a dad, period. Or at least, not so soon. We haven't even talked about moving in together."

"I've been ready for a long time. I was just waiting for you to be on the same page. I'm hoping our baby will improve my odds."

"The odds were always in your favor, Zak."

Her answer made him smile. And suddenly he knew moving in together wasn't enough. "This isn't the most romantic place or time, but I've got to ask you something."

"Yeah?" She raised her eyebrows uncertainly. "I hope you're not trying to back out of the visit to my parents?"

"Hell no. But when I meet your parents I'd like to be in a position to ask for their blessing. Will you marry me, Nadine?"

"Holy crap. I know you haven't had much sleep lately. Are you in your right mind?"

"Definitely."

"Then I guess my answer is yes."

May 10

AS ZAK ENTERED the Dew Drop, he was glad the others had gone ahead to save a table. The pub was more than usually busy, even for a Friday night. The entire town was in a celebrating mood. Sybil and Darby were home again, and safe. Everyone could go back to worrying if the creek would flood this June, and if they'd get another drought this summer.

That was the way nature worked here in the mountains. From one extreme to the other. Still, Zak had never wanted to live anywhere else.

"I ordered you a burger, no onions," Nadine told him as he pulled up his chair.

"Sounds perfect."

"Hey, Zak." Tiff was seated between Nadine and Kenny. She looked happy and exceptionally beautiful. Her long dark hair had been tamed into gentle, glossy waves, and she was wearing a new red lipstick that would make any man look twice.

He reached under the table for Nadine's hand.

"Beer's on me tonight." Kenny filled Zak's glass. "We've got lots to celebrate."

Zak couldn't agree more. He squeezed Nadine's hand,

then raised his glass. “So, what are we drinking to?”

“First, our sheriff’s skillful solving of the biggest kidnapping case this county has ever seen.”

“Sheriff *and* deputies *and* Bea,” Zak corrected. He noticed Nadine raised her glass but didn’t drink.

“Secondly,” Tiff continued, “we’re drinking to Clark Pittman moving out of Lost Trail. May we never see that hypocritical, conniving jackass again.”

Zak drank first, asked questions second. “So, what have I missed? Clark Pittman is moving?”

Tiff gave a satisfied smile. “Sure is. He left town last night. This morning we noticed a ‘For Sale’ sign was already up on his lawn.”

Zak was not sorry to see the last of the man. But the news surprised him. “I never thought he’d leave his son and granddaughter.”

“He and Justin had a big showdown a few days ago. Clark had been pressuring Justin and Geneva to move in with him. He’d actually put a deposit on the Penders’ estate home and acreage.”

Zak knew the place. The sprawling ranch home had to be at least five thousand square feet. And it sat on a pretty piece of land, outfitted for horses. “I’m guessing Clark figured Geneva needed her own pony?”

“Something like that. Anyway, Justin finally put his foot down with that man. He told him he was going to marry Debbie-Ann and she and her daughter were moving into his house."

Zak glanced at Nadine, who gave him a subtle wink. "That's good news. But I don't see why that would make Clark move. Don't he and Debbie-Ann get along?"

"Clark didn't approve of the marriage. But there were other factors, too."

The look that passed between Tiff and Kenny told Zak there was more to the story. "Do those other factors have to do with Martha Holmes switching babies so Justin ended up going home with the wrong parents?"

"They do," Kenny admitted.

Zak had always figured there was more to that story. But he'd just been a dispatcher back when Marsha Holmes took her life and posthumously assumed full responsibility for that long-ago crime.

"This town is better off without that man," Zak agreed. "Anything else you guys want to celebrate?"

"No," Tiff said. "But Nadine, I've never seen you take so long to drink that first beer before. What's up with that?"

Everyone looked at the full mug of beer that sat beside Nadine's almost-empty glass of water. Nadine raised her eyebrows and gave Zak a slow, sexy grin. "You want to tell them, Sheriff?"

He lifted his arm, so their linked hands were visible. "Nadine and I are getting married. Very soon. Before the baby arrives, for sure."

"Baby!" Tiff bounced in her chair and clasped her hands

together. “Oh, I’m so happy for you guys.” She jumped up and gave Nadine a hug, and then Zak.

Kenny reached across the table to shake their hands. “Man. I must be clueless. I work with you guys every day and I had no idea all this was in the offing.”

The conversation paused as Mari arrived with a tray laden with food. Burgers and fries for everyone except Nadine who’d order grilled chicken and spinach salad.

“I actually crave healthy food,” she told Tiff after being complimented for her healthy choice.

“Especially apples,” Zak said. He lifted the bun off the top of his burger. No onions. Life really was looking up these days.

The End

Author's Note

There are fifty-six counties in the great state of Montana. None of them is Bitterroot, the fictional county where this story takes place. In creating this setting I've taken some liberties with space and distance, placing my "new" county in a very isolated and sparsely-populated area somewhere between the real towns of Hamilton and Sula. Though there is a real ski hill named "Lost Trail," the town in my stories is as fictional as the county in which it is set.

Special thanks to Sergeant George Simpson with the Polson Police Department for so generously answering my questions regarding law enforcement and crime investigations in the state of Montana. Forgive me the creative license I have taken with those answers.

Thanks also to Jane, Meghan, Lee, Nikki, Helen and Marlene, the talented team at Tule Publishing who help turn my raw material into a polished, published novel.

If you enjoyed this book, please leave a review at your favorite online retailer! Even if it's just a sentence or two it makes all the difference.

Thanks for reading *Bitter Sweet* by C.J. Carmichael!

Discover your next romance at TulePublishing.com.

Bitter Root Mystery Series

On the surface Lost Trail, Montana is a picture-perfect western town offering beautiful mountain scenery and a simple way of life revolving around the local ranches as well as a nearby ski resort. But thirty-year old Tiff Masterson and her former school-chum Zak Waller—dispatcher at the local Sheriff's office—know there is darkness in this town, too, an evil with roots that neither of them fully understand.

Book 1: *Bitter Roots*

Book 2: *Bitter Truth*

Book 3: *Bitter End*

Book 4: *Bitter Sweet*

Available now at your favorite online retailer!

More books by C.J. Carmichael

The Carrigans of the Circle C series

Book 1: Promise Me, Cowboy

Book 2: Good Together

Book 3: Close to Her Heart

Book 4: Snowbound in Montana

Book 5: A Cowgirl's Christmas

Book 6: A Bramble House Christmas

Available now at your favorite online retailer!

About the Author

USA Today Bestselling author C. J. Carmichael has written over 50 novels with more than three million copies in print. She has been nominated for the *RT Bookclub's* Career Achievement in Romantic Suspense award, and is a three time nominee for the *Romance Writers of America* RITA Award.

Visit C.J.'s website at CJCarmichael.com

Thank you for reading

Bitter Sweet

If you enjoyed this book, you can find more from all our great authors at TulePublishing.com, or from your favorite online retailer.

Made in United States
North Haven, CT
22 July 2024

55289557R10183